rhcbooks.com

ISBN 978-0-7364-4338-8 (hardcover)
ISBN 978-0-7364-4339-5 (paperback)

Printed in the United States of America

10 9 8 7 6 5 4 3 2 1

DISNEY STRANGE WORLD

The Junior Novelization

Adapted by Erin Falligant

Random House 🏠 New York

Prologue

*B*eneath a misty sky, the humble but happy city of Avalonia lay trapped within a ring of never-ending mountains. Many determined pioneers had tried to conquer the deadly peaks. All had failed.

Only one man was brave enough and strong enough to find a path across the dangerous, rocky terrain: *Jaeger Clade.*

The toughest, most adventurous explorer in Avalonia, Jaeger Clade knew that it was his destiny to discover what existed beyond the mountains. After he married Penelope and they welcomed a baby boy, Jaeger longed to share that legacy with his son, Searcher. Together, they would slay the mountains. Nothing would stand in their way!

But as Searcher grew older, he was easily distracted by other things. He preferred studying plants to climbing mountains. Still, Jaeger pushed his son to do what others hadn't done before—what others *couldn't* do.

If Jaeger had his way, he and Searcher would prove to Avalonia and to the world that they were the incredible, *exceptional* Clades!

Chapter One

*F*ourteen-year-old Searcher trudged along the mountain path, struggling to follow his father under the weight of his pack. He stopped to take a breath as Jaeger powered ahead.

"Dad," Searcher said, breathing heavily. "We've been going like this for months. I mean, look at your crew. They're exhausted." He pointed to the group of weary explorers trailing behind them.

Jaeger looked over his shoulder at Searcher. His eyes glowered beneath bushy eyebrows, as thick and unruly as the moustache marching across his face. "Searcher, they don't build statues for people who *almost* make it past the mountains," he grumbled.

"But, Dad—" Searcher argued.

"No more bellyaching," Jaeger interrupted. "Now, keep up. You've been dragging your feet, too."

"That's easy for you to say," Searcher mumbled.

"You're not the one carrying a backpack the size of you."

"What was that?" Jaeger called.

"Nothing," Searcher said under his breath. He heaved the pack higher on his shoulders and tried to keep pace with Jaeger and the expedition team as they trekked across the mountain. But the wind howled, and the falling snow made the trail slippery.

When they rounded a bend, the team stopped suddenly. An enormous cavern opened before them. Inside, what resembled large, icy stalagmites seemed to be growing out of the ground, pointy tips down.

One of the crew members hurried ahead of the group, sighing with relief. He huddled just inside the cave, where he was protected from the harsh, icy wind. "Shelter! This is exactly what we need. Talk about a lifesaver!" he cried, his voice echoing through the cavern.

Over the crew member's head, an enormous, jagged icicle trembled . . . and then it came crashing down. *Thwunk!*

The expedition crew gasped and covered their eyes. Was he . . . dead?

The crew member peered out from behind the

wedge of ice, which had missed him by a hair. His face was pale with shock.

Jaeger scowled. "Die on your own time," he grumbled, keeping his voice low to avoid disturbing the thousands of remaining icicles that quivered on the ceiling. "Let's move." He signaled for silence and slowly entered the chasm.

Searcher met the eyes of the young explorer standing next to him. Callisto Mal was one of the youngest and bravest members of Jaeger's team. "Your dad's intense, Baby Clade," Callisto whispered to Searcher, her eyes sparkling with admiration.

"You have no idea," he whispered back with a tinge of irritation.

Searcher, Callisto, and the rest of the crew followed Jaeger, treading lightly.

But as Searcher wound his way through the fallen icicles, he spotted something in the snow—something green. He stepped around a large column of ice and found a collection of strange plants growing out of the snow. Round glowing pods grew under the large leaves.

"What the . . . ?" Searcher wondered aloud. He had never seen greenery quite like this. He looked closer, observing how the pods seemed to be buzzing with energy.

As he extended his fingers toward the glowing pods, the fur around his hood stood up straight with static electricity.

"Whoa!" he said, reaching closer. "What are you?"

Zzz! The plant zapped him with a spark.

"Ow!" Searcher cried—too loudly.

As Searcher's voice echoed through the chasm, Jaeger whirled around and glared at his son. What had Searcher just done?

A noise rumbled overhead.

"Run!" Jaeger ordered.

As icicles fell from the cliffs above, the crew raced forward—dodging the sharp daggers. Jaeger turned to see his son running to catch up. But suddenly, the floor collapsed beneath the teenager's feet.

"Searcher!" Jaeger cried as his son plummeted into the crevasse.

Searcher tried to grab on to a ledge, but his gloves slid uselessly across the slippery surface.

Jaeger quickly jammed an anchor into the icy wall, looped a rope around his waist, and leaped after his son. Swinging his ice picks, Jaeger bounded across falling ice chunks as he tried to reach Searcher, who continued to fall down, down, down. Jaeger pushed off one last ice chunk, launching his body toward his son. He reached out his hand, and Searcher grabbed it just in time. Holding on tight to his son, Jaeger swung them both to a safe ledge.

Searcher watched heavy blocks of ice sail past them into the abyss below. As he caught his breath, he looked up at his father with gratitude. But all he saw in Jaeger's eyes was disappointment.

"Come on, Searcher, use your head," Jaeger grumbled. "You're embarrassing me out here."

"Sorry, okay?" Searcher shot back, not sounding the least bit apologetic. Didn't his dad realize they could have died back there?

Without another word, Jaeger and Searcher climbed to rejoin the crew.

When Jaeger reached the group, a beam of light suddenly warmed the back of his neck. He turned to see a breathtakingly beautiful skyline of never-ending mountains. His stern expression softened into a smile.

"All right, everybody," Jaeger announced. "Let's get going. What lies beyond that horizon is Avalonia's future and our glory!"

"Uh, Dad?" said Searcher from behind him. He had just spotted something equally amazing. "What about these plants?"

Jaeger followed Searcher's gaze to a newly exposed cave filled with green plants that seemed alive with electricity. Power surged throughout the cave, sparking and flickering.

The rest of the team stared at the plants with awe. But Jaeger didn't seem the least bit impressed.

"We're explorers, Searcher, not gardeners," he said. "Let's move." He turned and began marching in the other direction.

But Searcher's feet remained glued to the ground. He studied the plants sparking with electricity. Whatever they were, he knew they were important— and that he had just made an amazing discovery.

"Wait, there's literally power surging through them," Searcher called after his father. "Who knows what this could mean for Avalonia. We need to take them back."

The crew looked on silently as Jaeger took this in. Nobody had ever challenged Jaeger Clade. He leaped down to where Searcher stood and towered over his son.

"Avalonia doesn't need sparkly plants," he growled. "What Avalonia needs is to expand beyond these mountains, and we are the ones meant to lead them there."

"Yes, Dad," Searcher started. "But—"

"No buts," Jaeger said, stomping his boot. "This is what I trained you for. This is our legacy."

Searcher shook his head. "No, Dad," he said firmly. "It's yours."

Jaeger was spitting mad now. "Enough of this!" he roared, grabbing Searcher's arm. "You're my son!"

"But I'm not you!" Searcher countered. He wrenched his arm from his father's grip.

Hurt crept across Jaeger's face, but only for a moment. Searcher held his father's stony gaze, not backing down.

Callisto cleared her throat and stepped forward. "Um, I think Baby Clade's right," she said, gesturing toward Searcher.

Jaeger raised his eyebrows. "Callisto?"

Callisto looked at the glowing plants that pulsed with energy inside the cave. "We don't actually know what's past these mountains," she said. "But these plants here—they're real. They could be the key to Avalonia's future. I think we have an obligation to bring them back."

As Jaeger studied the faces of his crew, he couldn't believe what he was seeing. They all seemed to be supporting Searcher! "What a waste," he scoffed. He turned his back on Searcher and the crew and stormed away.

"Jaeger?" Callisto called after him as he marched

toward the mountains on his own. "Jaeger, come back! You can't survive out there alone!"

Searcher's heart sank as he watched his father disappear into the mist. Would he ever see him again?

Chapter Two

Twenty-five years later, Searcher sipped coffee on his front porch and breathed in the fresh air. Searcher was now a farmer of Pando, the plant with the glowing pods that he had found in the mountains. Now his tidy rows of Pando stretched out across Clade Farms as far as the eye could see, the pods buzzing with energy.

A delivery boy approached on a vehicle that flew low to the ground as it sped along.

"Morning, Mr. Clade!" the delivery boy called, tossing a newspaper at Searcher's feet.

Searcher picked up the newspaper and dusted it off. "Rory, Mr. Clade was my dad's name," he reminded the boy. "Call me Searcher."

"Okay, Mr. Clade," the boy shouted as he raced off to his next delivery. "Tell Ethan I said hi!"

Searcher waved and then peered up toward his

teenage son's bedroom window. Time to get Ethan out of bed!

A few minutes later, Searcher stepped into Ethan's bedroom, balancing a plate of breakfast in his hand. A snoring lump lay beneath the colorful patchwork quilt. Searcher looked around the messy room and spotted a pulp magazine with an old photo of Jaeger Clade on the cover. He tiptoed to the magazine and flipped it over so he didn't have to see his father's face.

"Ethan? Hey, bud. Time to wake up," said Searcher. He gently pulled at the quilt. But instead of stirring Ethan, Searcher woke a furry beast. Legend, the family dog, shot out from beneath the quilt. He was as fast on three legs as most dogs on four. In an instant, he licked Searcher's face with his slobbery tongue.

"Legend, stop it!" cried Searcher, pushing the dog away. "No tongue! *No* tongue!"

Legend stopped but quickly became distracted by another tasty treat: Ethan's breakfast.

"Ah, Legend, stop!" Searcher cried as the dog licked the plate clean. "Ugh."

Hearing giggles, Searcher looked up and found his wife, Meridian, and their son laughing at him as they peeked out from beneath Ethan's quilt.

"You two think you're funny," Searcher said with a smirk.

"Are we funny, Ethan?" she asked, wrapping an arm around his shoulders.

"We're pretty hysterical, Mom," Ethan confirmed.

"You know what? Just for that, you two can make your own breakfasts," Searcher teased, shoving the slobbery plate toward them. He crossed his arms, pretending to be upset. But he could barely contain his smile.

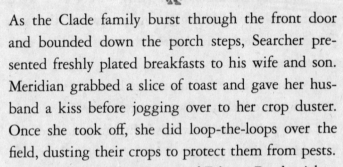

As the Clade family burst through the front door and bounded down the porch steps, Searcher presented freshly plated breakfasts to his wife and son. Meridian grabbed a slice of toast and gave her husband a kiss before jogging over to her crop duster. Once she took off, she did loop-the-loops over the field, dusting their crops to protect them from pests.

Down below, Searcher tossed Ethan a Pando picker, and they launched into morning chores, side by side.

Searcher found no greater joy than harvesting Pando pods with his son. They used the sharp blades of their Pando pickers to trim the ripest pods off the plant, dropping the pods into a basket before moving on to the next stalk. When the basket became too heavy, they carried it together. Once they'd filled their basket to the brim, they worked together to sort and package the pods to sell to their community.

As they worked, Searcher stole quick, proud glances at Ethan. His son was becoming quite the farmer. Together, they kept Clade Farms going strong, a legacy that Searcher could pass down to his son.

But as Searcher stared down a very messy row of Pando plants that the teenager had neglected, he noticed that Ethan still had a lot to learn.

"Looks like someone forgot to weed these rows," Searcher said, nudging Ethan's arm.

"Dad," Ethan argued playfully, "what is a weed other than just a plant growing somewhere that you find inconvenient?" He petted the vine tenderly, as if to comfort it.

Searcher grinned. "I appreciate how clever you are. But you know what I'd appreciate more?"

"If I pulled some weeds," Ethan conceded, his shoulders slumping.

"See?" Searcher said with satisfaction. "So clever."

As he watched Ethan get to work on the weeds, Meridian called his name. Searcher looked behind him and saw his wife's crop duster hovering over an adjacent field.

He ran over and stood beneath the lingering plane. "What's up?" he called to Meridian.

"My Pando engine stalled out," she answered. "Can you give me a hand?" She tossed him a rope, and he helped her down to the ground.

"Too much hotdogging?" he asked as Meridian pulled off her goggles.

She grinned. "Is there such a thing?" She hopped out of the pilot's seat and began inspecting the plane.

"Hmm," he said. "Pando battery's dead."

Searcher pointed to the battery hub, which looked dark and dull. He pulled out the battery and gently touched the Pando pods inside. No sparks.

Meridian's forehead wrinkled. "That doesn't make any sense. I picked those pods an hour ago."

Searcher dumped the spent pods into his hand. "Pests must be getting into the root system again," he said. He plucked fresh pods off a nearby plant and installed them in the hub, good as new.

"I'll give our fields some extra love as soon as I get the duster back in the air," Meridian promised.

A car horn sounded in the distance.

"Hey, the crew's here!" said Searcher, smiling broadly.

"*Ethan's* crew," Meridian corrected him as he handed her the refreshed battery hub. "Not *your* crew."

But Searcher was already hurrying toward the sound of the horn. "Yeah," he said over his shoulder, "but his friends love me!"

"We talked about this!" Meridian called after him. "Ethan's a teenager. Boundaries!"

By then, Searcher was halfway across the field. "Yeah, yeah," he said quickly. "Boundaries. Got it!"

Beep, beep, beep!

A rattly, run-down air buggy bounced along the driveway. Ethan's friend Kardez waved from the driver's seat. Another friend, Azimuth, leaned out from the back, red hair blowing in the wind.

"Ethan! Ethan!" Kardez called as he extracted his large frame from the buggy.

"Kardez, Kardez, what?" Ethan replied, grinning as he leaped over the wooden fence.

"We just came back from the game shop," Kardez announced. "The special edition of Primal Outpost just dropped. They sold out in fifteen minutes!" He held up a pack of hexagonal game cards. Azimuth flashed a pack, too—and a satisfied smile.

"What?" Ethan slapped a hand to his forehead. "They sold out already? I knew I should have camped out!"

"Don't worry," someone called from inside the vehicle. "We didn't forget about you."

Diazo popped up from the back of the buggy. With his shock of blonde hair and golden skin, Diazo could have been the front man of a teenage boy band.

"Oh, uh, hey, Diazo," Ethan stammered, his cheeks flushing. "I didn't see you there. Not that you're not noticeable. I just, um . . . it was just, uh . . . What's up? Hey." He crossed his arms and leaned awkwardly against the fence.

Diazo hopped out of the buggy and held up two card packs. "I knew you had to work this morning," he said, "so I made sure we grabbed you a pack."

"You did?" said Ethan. "That's . . . that's really sweet."

"Ugh, okay," said Azimuth impatiently. "We have allotted three to five minutes of cute flirtation. Can we open our packs already?"

"Yo, I hear the new creatures are *steep*!" said Kardez.

They tore open their packs in a flurry of crinkly paper.

"Medic," said Azimuth, presenting a role card with a red cross.

"Cook," Kardez declared, holding up his own card. "Yesss! I'm gonna make some *stuff*. . ."

But when Ethan ripped open his pack, he sank like a deflated balloon. "Farmer," he mumbled, spotting the figure with a hoe. "Uff."

Diazo offered Ethan his card. "Here," he said, "I'll trade you. This one feels more *Ethan* to me."

The card showed a figure holding a flag—the explorer! It was the exact role card Ethan wanted. How had Diazo known?

They shared a smile, and then Diazo asked, "Isn't your grandpa, like, a famous explorer? Maybe it's in your blood." Diazo pointed at the explorer card. "He kind of looks like you, except for that. . . ." He plucked Ethan's hat off his head and darted off playfully.

While Ethan chased after Diazo, Kardez and Azimuth looked at each other with an expression that said "Aren't they adorable?"

Diazo finally stopped running and tossed Ethan's hat back. That's when Searcher strolled up to the fence from the Pando field. "Hey, gang, what's the haps?" he said with a smile.

Ethan grimaced. "Dad, what are you doing?" He hurried toward Searcher as if he could stop whatever was about to happen.

"Ooh, is this him?" Searcher whispered to Ethan, much too loudly.

"Dad," Ethan whispered through a forced smile, pleading with his eyes for Searcher to go on his merry way.

But it was too late. Searcher half climbed, half tripped over the fence and marched toward Diazo. Legend had taken the fence in a single bound and was already loving up Diazo as if he were an old friend.

Searcher held out his hand. "Sup? I'm Ethan's dad, Searcher. You must be Diazo. He talks about you *all* the time."

"Not *all* the time," Ethan said quickly. "Maybe

sometimes—or on occasion." He shrank into himself as if trying to disappear.

"So, Diazo," Searcher went on, "tell me about yourself."

Ethan barked a nervous laugh. "That's not really necessary."

"Are you into farming?" asked Searcher. "Because Ethan is an amazing farmer. You should see him out here. He's strong, smart, super cool—or as you kids say, *steep*!"

"Wow," said Azimuth, stifling a laugh.

"Oh-kay," said Ethan, stepping between Searcher and Diazo. "Don't we have deliveries to make?" he asked his dad.

"Oh yeah," Searcher said as his son pulled him away.

"Sorry, guys," Ethan said in a strained voice. "Gotta go now. Apologies that my dad is so . . . Dad."

With one nudge from Ethan, Searcher tripped headfirst over the fence. Ethan followed him over and waved. "Bye!" He led his dad back through the fields, away from the air buggy, away from Diazo.

"Bye, Ethan!" his friends called. "Farewell, Ethan! Bye, Ethan's dad!"

Searcher gave a hearty wave before turning to Ethan. "Hey, Diazo seems cool," he said with a grin. "I see why you like him."

"Please stop talking," Ethan said.

But Searcher went on. "I remember my first crush," he said dreamily. "She had braces. I did, too. And then one time we got stuck—ooh, it wasn't such a bad thing!"

Ethan pressed his hands to his ears. "Stop talking, stop talking, stop talking!" he groaned. "Ugh, what is happening to my life?"

That afternoon, Searcher, Ethan, and Legend rode the family's Pando-fueled truck into town. Over the past twenty-five years, Avalonia had changed greatly, thanks to the plants Searcher had discovered in the mountains. Pando pods now powered all sorts of modern inventions: Airships whizzed overhead. Cars, trains, and boats sped along the streets and waterways. Bright streetlamps lit the city, all powered by Pando.

Townspeople greeted Searcher and Ethan as they delivered boxes of Pando pods labeled with the Clade Farms logo. Everyone was eager to compliment Ethan for how much he was like his father, which made Searcher surge with pride.

At last, Searcher pulled his truck up to the town square, with one last crate of pods to deliver. Ethan and Legend jumped out and began to play fetch beneath the towering statues that adorned the square. Each statue honored an important figure from Avalonia—including none other than Searcher himself, whose discovery of Pando had made him the town hero.

Searcher handed the crate of pods to his friend Ro and closed the tailgate. Then he leaned against the truck with satisfaction and watched his son play.

"Legend!" Ethan called, throwing the stick toward Searcher's statue. "Go get it! Good boy!"

Legend bounded after the stick and obediently brought it back to Ethan, who paused to look up at another statue—one honoring Jaeger Clade, the legendary explorer who had never returned from his mountain expedition.

"Would you look at that," Ro remarked to Searcher. "Three generations of Clades. I wonder which one your son will take after."

"I think that's pretty obvious," Searcher said, looking at Ro with an amused expression. Ethan was his father's son! How could he possibly have anything in common with the grandfather he had never met?

But when Searcher glanced at Ethan, he imagined him transforming into a spitting image of Jaeger Clade. He could almost hear his father's voice chiding him: "You know he's gonna grow up to be just like me and leave you like I did! Ha ha ha!"

"Searcher, you okay?" asked Ro, studying Searcher's pale face.

Searcher shivered and shook off the horrifying vision. "Yep! Yeah, we'll see you next week, Ro!" He turned and called out to his son. "Come on, Ethan! Let's go."

They summoned Legend into the truck and buckled their seat belts. As Searcher adjusted his rearview mirror, he caught one last glimpse of Jaeger's statue.

Ethan glanced at Searcher. "You know, I bet your dad would be really proud of everything you've accomplished," he said.

Searcher quickly looked away from the mirror. "You clearly don't know anything about your grandpa," he said with a shrug and a sarcastic chuckle.

"I mean, I would if you ever talked about him," said Ethan. "Dad, he's my grandfather. I want to know about him—from you."

Searcher took a deep breath. "Everyone thinks of Jaeger Clade as this amazing hero," he started, "but that's only because they didn't have him as a father. To me, he was just a . . . really bad dad. He didn't care about me. He only cared about conquering those mountains." Searcher held his hand to Ethan's cheek. "I only care about you, our family, and our farm."

Ethan looked up with a smile. "Well, I guess that's what makes you a pretty good dad," he said.

Searcher's ears perked up. "Wait, what was that?"

Ethan froze, realizing that his dad was about to get weird again. "Nothing!" he said, lying. "I opened my mouth, and no words came out."

"No, no, I heard you," he said, grinning with satisfaction as he started the truck.

"Pretty good!" Ethan said, trying to downplay the compliment he'd just given his father. "*Pretty* good!"

Searcher's eyes sparkled with mischief as he opened the truck's windows and pulled out of the town square. "My son thinks I'm an amazing dad!" he hollered for the entire town to hear.

Legend howled with delight, and Searcher joined him. Ethan sank in his seat in utter embarrassment as they made their way home.

Chapter Three

*T*hat night, as the Clades were making dinner, Meridian walked over to the record player and dropped the needle. Music rang out from the speaker as she took Searcher's hand, inviting him to dance with her.

Ethan looked on with mock horror as his parents twirled across the kitchen floor. When Meridian bent Searcher backward in a dip, Ethan pretended to be grossed out. "I'm right here!" he cried. But he couldn't help laughing when Legend reared up on his hind legs, begging to be Ethan's dance partner.

That's when the house suddenly began to shake.

Something sank low in the sky and hovered overhead—something very large and very loud.

"What the . . . ," Meridian said under her breath. She raced out the front door, with Searcher and Ethan close behind.

There, looming above the Pando fields, was a

state-of-the-art flying ship. The massive green airship nearly dwarfed the house as it lowered toward the ground.

Ethan sucked in his breath. "Whoa," he said, his locs rippling from the *whoosh* of the propellors. "What kind of airship is that?"

"I don't know," Meridian hollered above the din. "I've never seen anything like it."

As the ship settled on the field, Searcher raced toward it, waving his oven mitts in the air. "Hey!" he hollered. "What are you doing? No, you're damaging our crops!"

His voice was drowned out by a hydraulic whir. As the airship landed with a *thud,* the ship's metal hull opened, and a walkway dropped down. In a burst of light, a tall, imposing woman emerged from the ship with her crew close behind.

"Baby Clade!" the woman called in greeting. "How long has it been, huh?"

Searcher squinted. "Callisto?"

"You *know* her?" Ethan asked in disbelief.

"Yeah." Searcher nodded. "She used to work with my dad."

"What is the leader of Avalonia doing in our front yard?" Meridian asked aloud. Searcher shrugged, equally baffled.

President Callisto Mal approached them, flanked

by two crew members. Pulk, tall and thin in a green flight suit, wore long braids and an expression that said, "Don't mess with me." Hardy was shorter, but his beefy arms and broad chest spoke for themselves.

"Get in here!" Callisto said, throwing her arms out. "So good to see you, man!" Before Searcher could move, she pulled him in for a bear hug. Then she turned to his family and offered them hearty handshakes. "You must be Meridian. So lovely to meet you. And Ethan, the future of Clade Farms. Your dad must be so proud of you, man!"

Ethan gave an uneasy laugh.

Callisto waved toward the airship. "Oh, hey, is it okay if we park the *Venture* here? You know, I can tell my pilot to move it. It's not a big deal. . . . I mean, it *is* a big deal, but it's not a big deal."

"No, no, no," Meridian said quickly. "It's fine."

Ethan's eyes grew wide as he scanned the enormous airship. "Can the *Venture* fly over the mountains?" he blurted.

Searcher squinted at his son. Meridian was surprised, too. Since when did Ethan have any interest in the mountains?

"Sorry," Callisto said. "Nothing can fly that high." She gazed at the looming peaks in the distance and then winked at Ethan. "Not yet, anyways."

Ethan grinned.

Callisto chuckled. "But that's not why I'm here."

"Why *are* you here?" Searcher asked.

Her expression turned serious. "There's something I need to show you."

A short while later, Callisto plunked a wooden crate onto the Clade's dinner table. It was full of black, rotting Pando plants.

Searcher reached into the crate. "Where did you find these?" he asked, lifting a shriveled pod from the crate.

"It started in the Northeast territory," Callisto explained, "and has been spreading like wildfire ever since. According to our estimates, every crop will be infected within a month—including your farm."

Searcher and Meridian shared a concerned look.

"Searcher, I'm mounting an expedition to save Pando," Callisto announced. "And I want you to come with me."

Searcher spit out a mouthful of water. "Callisto, I don't go on expeditions," he said. "I'm not my father."

A sober expression crossed Callisto's face. "Yeah, he didn't come back. You did. And you brought back a miracle. And now there's something wrong with it."

Feeling overwhelmed, Searcher stepped toward the window and gazed at his fields. "Look at how they glow out there," he marveled as the plants pulsed with energy. "It's like a heartbeat, isn't it?"

Callisto joined him at the window. "Searcher, I was there when you found Pando," she reminded him. "Look what it's given us. Airships. The lights in our homes. But most importantly, it showed us our future wasn't out there somewhere"—she gestured toward the mountains—"but here. Pando's dying, Searcher. You and I . . . we have an obligation to save it."

His eyes remained glued to his healthy, glowing crops. How long would they stay that way? When he turned back toward Ethan, Searcher knew what he had to do. He *had* to try to save Pando—for himself, for Avalonia, and for Ethan.

Searcher took a deep breath. "Okay," he said.

"Yes!" cried Ethan. "When do we head out?"

Searcher raised his hand. "Whoa, hold up," he said. "You're not coming with me."

Ethan's face fell. "But we do *everything* together!"

"Not this," said Searcher firmly.

Ethan pointed toward the farm fields. "Then what's the point of you showing me how to grow Pando my whole life?"

"So you can take over the farm," said Searcher.

Ethan pressed his fingers to his temples. "But this is so much more important!" he cried.

"No," said Searcher.

"But, Dad . . ."

Searcher held up his hand again. "I will not risk your life. Not now, not ever."

When Ethan saw that his dad's mind was made up, he let out an exasperated sigh. Then he stomped up the stairs and closed his bedroom door behind him.

"Ethan!" Searcher called. "Ethan!"

Before he could chase after him, Callisto stopped him. "Unfortunately, Searcher, every second we delay puts Avalonia in graver danger."

Searcher peered up the stairs but then nodded. "I'll go get my things."

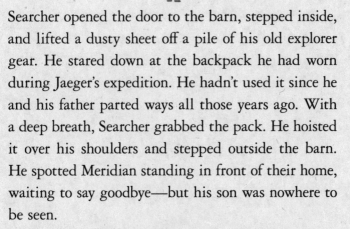

Searcher opened the door to the barn, stepped inside, and lifted a dusty sheet off a pile of his old explorer gear. He stared down at the backpack he had worn during Jaeger's expedition. He hadn't used it since he and his father parted ways all those years ago. With a deep breath, Searcher grabbed the pack. He hoisted it over his shoulders and stepped outside the barn. He spotted Meridian standing in front of their home, waiting to say goodbye—but his son was nowhere to be seen.

Searcher sighed and looked up at Ethan's window. "I hate leaving him like this," he said.

"He'll be fine once he cools down a bit," Meridian said, reassuring him.

"Are *you* gonna be okay?" he asked, studying her expression.

She smiled and touched her husband's face. "Go save our farm," she said firmly. "We'll be fine."

As Searcher started up the metal walkway of the ship, he cast one more look over his shoulder at Meridian and the farm he loved. When she blew him a kiss, he caught it—just as the metal hull closed with a *clang*.

Chapter Four

*T*he *Venture*'s Pando-powered engine revved, and the propellors began to whir. Moments later, the airship rose high above the glowing Pando plants of Searcher's farm. Then it veered toward the mountains in the distance.

Callisto wasted no time gathering Searcher and the crew to prepare for the mission. As everyone took their seats, a bearded and burly crew member sitting next to Searcher introduced himself.

"Mr. Clade, it's great to meet you," Caspian said. "I'm a huge fan—"

"Oh, thank you," Searcher said.

"Of your dad," Caspian continued. "Do you think you could forge his autograph?" He thrust a magazine into Searcher's hands.

Searcher looked down. There was that famous photo of his father's face looking up at him once again.

Before Searcher could say a word, Pulk signaled for silence. "All right, everyone, listen up!" she announced. "Your president is about to speak."

Callisto stepped up to face the crew. "Thank you, Captain Pulk." She gestured toward a projection screen that showed a diagram of Pando plants growing out of the dirt. Two of the plants were crossed out with big red Xs.

"Though Pando seems to be thousands of plants here on the surface," Callisto said, "underground it is actually a singular organism with an interconnected root system." She clicked to the next image, which showed the plants' long roots joining together underground. "We believe whatever's making Pando sick is attacking it deep within this system, at its heart."

Callisto clicked to a map of Avalonia's Pando crops and tapped her pointer stick at an area deep in the mountains. "Three weeks ago, Captain Pulk here tracked the roots out to the Atlas range, where they suddenly took a turn downward," she explained. She clicked to a photo of Pulk leading their team on a dig, and then to an image of Pulk and the team leaping to safety as the earth crumbled beneath them.

"They started excavating—but the ground gave out, revealing an even bigger mystery." Callisto paused and rolled up the projection screen to reveal what lay beyond the window of the airship: an enormous hole in the earth below. "Our mission is to follow these roots until we reach the heart of Pando—and stop whatever's harming it."

Searcher approached the window and gaped at the scene before him. "So how far does it go down?" he asked Callisto.

She hesitated. "We're not sure. But Avalonia's future depends on us finding out."

The *Venture*'s pilot leaned toward Searcher. Duffle was a tall, thin man whose moustache seemed to wrap all the way across his face. "*Psst,* Clade," he said. "Listen, we got no idea what's down there, so if you wanna back out, I could drop you off."

"Wait, seriously?" said Searcher, touched by the crew member's concern.

Duffle burst into laughter. "Nah, I'm just messing with ya!" he said. "Look at your face! We need you to figure this out, or we're doomed. Doomed!" He said the word with something resembling glee.

"Lieutenant Duffle," Pulk said sternly, "if you're done messing with Mr. Clade, can you please earn your paycheck and fly us down?"

"Yes, Captain Pulk," said Duffle, turning back to the controls.

As the ship descended, its bright headlights cut through the dark void and illuminated long strings of glowing Pando roots lining the cavern.

From the cockpit, Searcher sucked in his breath at the sight of the roots. They grew thick and strong, snaking across the walls and dangling toward the mysterious depths below. He stepped out on deck for a closer look.

Searcher smiled, hearing the sound of electricity thrumming through the roots like a heartbeat. "Oh, wow," he murmured. "It's beautiful."

Callisto stepped up beside him. "I wish everyone in Avalonia could see this," she said.

As they gazed up at the pulsing roots, a voice rang out from overhead.

"Searcher! Searcher!"

"What is that?" cried Searcher, gripping the rail.

"Whatever it is," said Callisto, "it knows your name."

They glanced up to see Meridian's crop duster descending rapidly toward them. "Searcher!" called the voice again.

"Meridian?" Searcher shaded his eyes against the lights of the plane. "What are you doing down here?"

"I've been trying to flag you down for the last four hours," Meridian cried. "Our son . . . is on . . . your ship!"

"What did she just say?" asked Searcher, shouting against the buzz of the plane's propellers. "Honey, what are you saying? What is she saying?" He turned toward Callisto, hoping she had understood.

"She said your *son* is on our ship," Pulk answered from behind Searcher. The crew member wasn't alone. Pulk had a firm grip on Ethan's arm.

"Hey, Mom!" Ethan shouted, gazing up.

"Ethan?" said Searcher incredulously.

"Oh, hey, Dad," said Ethan, waving as if they had just run into each other in a field back home.

Before Searcher could speak, a furry monster bounded toward him, leaped into his arms, and licked his face. "Ugh, and you brought the dog?" Searcher cried, holding Legend tight. "What are you doing here?"

Ethan raised his palms. "Look, Dad, I just want to help."

Searcher's face softened. "Ethan, we talked about this. I can't. I need you to take care of the farm while I'm gone." He handed Legend over to Ethan. "Now, please, go home with Mom."

"Wait, but, Dad—" Ethan started. No sooner had the words left his mouth than . . .

Crunch! Something struck the ship. The *Venture* lurched sideways. Searcher felt the *whoosh* of wings as a creature flew overhead. He ducked, pulling Ethan behind him.

Callisto looked up as a red blur swooped toward them, screeching. As more winged creatures dove toward the ship, she took charge. "Head inside!" she ordered. "I've got this!"

She drew two daggers from her belt and leaped off the deck, fighting off the flying beasts. As she dropped to the roof of the ship, more creatures appeared—scads of them. Callisto hollered one word to Searcher: "Run!"

Searcher hurried Ethan and Legend toward the cockpit door. Before they could reach it, a creature landed, blocking their path. It rose up, fiercely flapping its wings.

"Hey! Razor face!" Callisto called to the sharp-nosed creature. "Yeah, come and get me!" She clashed her knives together, distracting the beast and allowing Ethan and Searcher to rush by unseen. Then Callisto dropped into the cockpit. "Duffle, get us out of here!" she cried.

Before the pilot could change course, a winged creature burst through the windshield, grabbed the pilot with its tail, and dragged him from the cockpit. Duffle's foot knocked the control panel, pushing a lever askew.

The damaged, pilotless *Venture* began to careen downward, nose first. Callisto couldn't reach the control panel. All she could do was hang on for dear life.

From above, Meridian saw the ship plummeting. She pushed the throttle of her plane and zoomed toward the *Venture*. Back and forth, she weaved through the flying beasts until she was neck and neck with the ship.

"What the—" said Callisto when Meridian appeared.

"Hold on!" cried Meridian.

Out on deck, Searcher gripped the rail with one hand and Ethan with the other. But as the *Venture* tilted sideways, Legend slid across the deck, barking excitedly.

"Legend!" Ethan cried.

Searcher let go of the rail and sailed toward Legend. "I got him!"

In the same moment, Meridian leaped from her stunt plane into the cockpit of the *Venture*. She raced to the control panel and tried to make sense of the countless rows of levers and buttons. But when she looked out the windshield and saw Ethan desperately clinging to the railing, she knew what she had to do. She grabbed the wheel and fought to steady the ship.

As the *Venture* broke through a tangle of Pando roots, Meridian saw that they were about to reach the bottom of the hole—but they were falling too fast.

"Brace yourself!" Meridian cried over the sound of the ship's alarms.

Down, down, down they plunged toward the cavern floor. And then they hit bottom.

But instead of crashing, the ship cut straight through the ground like a knife through butter. *Bloop!*

The *Venture* emerged in an entirely new world. Gone were the dark cavern walls. Everything in this world—the walls, sky, and floor—was a pale shade of red.

But the force of impact sent Searcher sliding straight off the ship's deck.

"Dad!" Ethan cried as Searcher fell, taking Legend with him.

"Ahhh!" Searcher gripped the dog as they plummeted toward a ridge of purple trees. Searcher bounced off a branch and then . . .

Plunk! He thumped softly onto the ground. The earth rippled like gelatin beneath him.

Searcher inspected his body, making sure nothing was broken. But he was fine. Perfectly fine. And Legend was, too.

"Dad!" Ethan cried from the deck of the *Venture,* which was still speeding across the crimson landscape.

"Ethan!" Searcher called.

The *Venture* continued on its crash course, skidding through a forest of orange and fuchsia trees. "We're coming in too hot!" Callisto cried to Meridian.

"I know!" Meridian said through gritted teeth. She veered left to graze a tree, using friction to slow the ship's speed. The *Venture* careened toward another tree and clipped that one, too.

"C'mon, *Venture*!" Meridian cried, willing the ship to slow down. "Hang in there!"

The ship plowed through smaller trees filled with bright purple clusters. Then she saw that the forest was on a cliff. And the *Venture* was sliding straight toward the edge of that cliff.

"Not today!" Meridian declared. She pushed a button, rocketing an anchor out of the ship. The anchor caught, slowing the *Venture* to a halt just feet from the cliffside.

As the ship rocked back and forth, Meridian blew out her breath. "Did you have any idea all of this was down here?" she asked.

Callisto shook her head. "Not at all." She swallowed hard. "We are definitely off the map now."

The two women gazed out the shattered windshield at this strange new place. They had survived—but their adventure had only just begun.

Chapter Five

From a hilltop nearby, Searcher watched the *Venture* skid to a stop—*finally*. "They're okay!" he cried to Legend. "And we're okay!"

The dog leaped with joy, knocking Searcher over before plastering his face with wet kisses.

"All right, all right," said Searcher, laughing as he pushed the dog's snout away. "I'm happy, too. Easy on the tongue. Easy on the tongue!"

He sat up, wiped his face, and took in the world around him. A river of red whalelike creatures gushed overhead. In the valley below, a tuft-headed animal loped toward its herd, and lanky, dinosaur-like beasts trod across the earth. This was a bizarre, beautiful place.

"Where in the world are we?" Searcher asked as a swarm of pinwheel-like bugs fluttered past.

Then he spotted something familiar snaking across

the ceiling: Pando roots. They were glowing, healthy, and strong. "Our little plant's a survivor," Searcher murmured to Legend.

But the dog had other things on his mind. One of the pinwheel-like bugs had caught his attention, and he pounced.

"Legend, leave it!" Searcher ordered. "We have no idea what that is. Get it out of your mouth!"

Searcher was so focused on Legend that he didn't realize something was watching *him,* too. In the bushes nearby, a creature lurked. Its burly body was covered head to toe in shaggy fur.

"All right, boy," said Searcher when Legend finally dropped the bug. "Let's get back to our family."

But when he pulled out a bandanna to wipe his brow, something grabbed it. Searcher whirled around to find a little blue blobby creature with a death grip on his bandanna.

"What the . . . ," Searcher said. He yanked, lifting the creature right off the ground. Its many limbs hung slack, as if it were playing dead.

Searcher leaned forward for a closer look. When he poked the blob's belly, the creature sprang to life, flapping its arm loose from Searcher's grip. Then it snatched the bandanna and began to run.

"Hey!" cried Searcher. Before he could take a step,

Legend took off after the little blue blob. "Legend, get back here!"

Legend chased the chattering creature as it hopped and scurried away.

Searcher chased Legend.

As the blue blob crested a hill, it waved to get the attention of something else—something *much* more menacing. An enormous, round purple beast rolled into view.

The little blue blob held up the bandanna and pointed in Searcher's direction. The round monster turned and rolled straight toward Searcher and Legend. They froze in their tracks before slowly stepping backward.

Suddenly, the beast opened its mouth, and long tentacles shot out. The snakelike tongues lunged for Searcher, ready to snatch him up.

"Ahhh!" Searcher cried, stumbling to the ground as he shielded Legend. He scooted away, but he couldn't escape. The tentacled creature was too fast!

Just then, something streaked overhead with a roar. The furry creature that had been spying from the bushes leaped over Searcher and landed between him and the tentacled beast. It held a strange contraption that blasted the monster with a stream of fire. As the beast rolled away in rapid retreat, the blue blob that had summoned it raced away, too, waving Searcher's bandanna like a flag of surrender.

Searcher studied the furry creature that had just saved his life. His voice trembled as he introduced himself. "Hi, hello. I'm a human being from the top world." As the monster stepped toward him, Searcher prattled on nervously. "You probably don't understand a word I'm saying, do you?"

Then he held his breath. Would the creature answer him—or attack him? Searcher squeezed Legend tightly.

The monster suddenly snorted and . . . spoke. "Of course I understand you," it grumbled. "What do you think I am? One of these mindless monsters?"

"Huh?" Searcher's eyebrows shot up in surprise.

"That's right, bub," said the creature. "You're in the presence of the one, the only"—it reached up and pulled off its furry costume—"Jaeger . . ."

Searcher stared at the gray-haired man with the long scraggly beard. His clothes were tattered, but he stood tall and strong. Searcher sucked in his breath. "Dad?" he cried.

Jaeger's jaw dropped. "Dad?" he repeated.

Ethan stood on the wing of the *Venture* and looked off in the distance, searching for his father. Meanwhile, Callisto gathered the crew on the entrance ramp. As the leader addressed the group, Ethan climbed down to listen, eager to find out how she planned to rescue Searcher.

"Okay, everyone," she began. "We are clearly in uncharted territory. I know you're all feeling scared." She looked around at the battered and bewildered group. "I am, too."

Caspian nodded. "I mighta peed my pants a little," he admitted to the crew member standing next to him.

"But the mission remains the same," Callisto continued. "We're here to save Pando. Okay? But before we can do that, we need to get our ship back into the air." She paused.

"What about my dad?" Ethan asked, looking from Callisto to his mother, who stood next to him. "Shouldn't we save him first? He's a farmer. You can't just leave him out there."

"No one's leaving anyone," Callisto said in a soothing voice. She looked into the teenager's pleading eyes. "I know you're worried about your dad, but I've seen him out in the field firsthand. He knows how to survive. If we want to do the same, our best bet is to retrieve him by air—which means fixing this ship *is* the priority."

"But that's gonna take way too long!" cried Ethan, his voice rising with panic.

"She's right, Ethan," Meridian said, laying a hand on her son's shoulder.

"What?" he exclaimed. How could his mother side with Callisto on this one?

"Babe, we have no idea what's out there," said Meridian. "The *Venture* is our safest option."

"But, Mom—"

"Honey," she said firmly, "why don't you go hang out in the cockpit while I help them with repairs?"

He grunted, realizing he couldn't win this battle.

Callisto nodded. "I promise you, Ethan, we're gonna save your dad." Then she turned to Meridian. "Thanks for the backup."

Meridian nodded. "I'm gonna hold you to that promise," she said, following Callisto around the side of the ship.

Pulk barked orders at the crew. "You have your assignments. Get moving! Caspian, can you keep an eye on Ethan?"

"Come on, Ethan!" he said, excited to have been given such an important duty. "We're going to have the best time! You like board games, right?" He walked ahead, gesturing for Ethan to follow. "We have best games: Rung and Rafters, Candy Jams, Battle Trip . . ."

Ethan glanced over his shoulder at a fleet of life-boat skiffs parked outside the *Venture*. He suddenly had an idea. . . .

"Nope, nope, no," Jaeger Clade was saying, his hands covering his ears. "Uh-uh. You're not my son."

"What?" Searcher couldn't believe his father was walking away from him—again, after all these years. "What are you talking about?" he cried, chasing after him.

"You're probably just some oddly shaped rock that my eyes want to believe is a person," Jaeger said as they emerged from the thicket. Legend raced close behind.

"I am *not* an oddly shaped rock," Searcher pro-tested, pointing his finger defiantly in his father's face. That's when he noticed he was standing next to a tall rock shaped an awful lot like him.

"That's exactly what an oddly shaped rock would say," Jaeger declared.

"Wow," said Searcher, throwing up his hands. This was going to be tougher than he'd thought. "Okay, well, would an oddly shaped rock know that you gave me a machete for my birthday?"

Jaeger chuckled to himself. "Classic Jaeger Clade," he said proudly.

"I was two!" shouted Searcher, exasperated.

Jaeger turned and studied Searcher again, as if he wasn't quite sure. . . .

"I'm *real,* Dad," said Searcher earnestly. "It's really me—your son, Searcher."

Jaeger's eyes softened with recognition. "Searcher?"

Searcher nodded.

"This . . . is . . . incredible!" cried Jaeger, taking his son in as if seeing him for the first time.

"I was thinking the same!" said Searcher. He stepped toward his father, ready for a hug.

But instead, he ran into the meaty hand that Jaeger had just thrust forward. Searcher shook his father's hand awkwardly.

"This means that flying machine that crashed is also real!" Jaeger said gleefully.

"Yeah?" Searcher's brow wrinkled with confusion.

"Well, let's get moving!" bellowed Jaeger, already darting ahead. "We got no time to lose!" He sprinted in the direction of the crashed airship.

"Whoa, wait! Wait!" Searcher raced after him. Then he spotted Legend—or at least *most* of Legend.

The dog's head was engulfed in some sort of man-eating plant, but his tail was wagging.

"Will you get that off your head?" Searcher cried, pulling the dog free. He hurried to catch up with Jaeger, with Legend barking happily beside him.

Chapter Six

"Dad! Dad?" Ethan called. He sped through the strange new world on a motorized skiff, laughing and loving every moment as he looked for his father. "Woo-hoo! This is way faster than our tractor. I gotta get me one of these!"

As he entered a forest, he dodged the glowing trees. Tall, slender, and blue, each grew out of a bulb at its base and had palmlike leaves at the top. And what was swinging from the branches? Chimpanzees?

Ethan slowed down to study the creatures. They looked more like sloths. Sparkly, star-shaped sloths. Except he'd never seen sloths move like these. As they swung quickly from tree to tree, each branch they touched began to glow.

Ethan laughed in wonder. As the trees thinned and he entered a clearing, he took it all in. But when he glanced at the path ahead, he saw that it was ending. At the edge of a cliff. Very soon.

Ethan skidded to a stop, swinging the rear of the skiff around just in time. As he caught his breath, he gazed out at the horizon. Purplish-red land formations rose all around him, dotted with clusters of pink trees.

"I can't believe it," Ethan murmured. "A vast undiscovered wilderness filled with fantastic creatures. This is just like Primal Outpost!"

Then the world beneath him started to rumble and shake. Ethan tumbled off his skiff onto the ground, except it wasn't the ground at all. He had parked on top of a flat, round, pinkish-white being. It flapped and fluttered like a giant manta ray.

As the creature rose, Ethan slid off its edge. "Ahhhhh!" He plunged down, bouncing off purple mushroomy blobs and landing on his back on the rubbery ground.

The flat creature flew away, joining several others just like it—and taking Ethan's skiff with them.

He thought again of his favorite game. "Okay," he admitted with a sigh, "this is nothing like Primal Outpost."

He pushed himself up and took a look around. He had fallen into a deep pit, with walls too steep to scale. The only way out seemed to be through a long, dark tunnel.

Ethan had to summon all his courage to enter it.

He pulled out the Primal Outpost card Diazo had given him and gazed at the brave explorer Diazo had compared him to. "You can do this, Ethan," he told himself. "Just be brave. It's in your blood."

Then he took a deep breath. He stepped into the tunnel. And he began to run.

"Aaaaaaaaaaaaaaahhh!" Ethan bellowed as he raced straight through to the other side.

When he emerged in a large cave, he leaned over, trying to catch his breath. "Okay," he said, looking again at his explorer card. He laughed with relief. "I'm alive. I did it." He tucked the card in his pocket and continued confidently through the winding cave.

As he walked, he pretended he was talking with Diazo. "Oh, hey, Diazo," he said. "How was my weekend? What did I do? Oh, yeah, I just ran through a nightmare tunnel to rescue my dad. No big deal. Yeah—"

A strange chirping sound stopped him in his tracks.

"Hello?" called Ethan.

He heard the sound again, close by this time. He glanced at his shadow on the cavern wall. Something was crawling up the bottom of his backpack. A spidery blob-like creature was creeping toward Ethan's head!

Ethan slowly turned, holding his breath. As the

blue blobby thing squealed, Ethan squawked. He tried to grab the alien blob. He ran in circles, trying to fling it from his pack. But it was stuck!

Ethan fell to his back, trying to flatten the creature against the ground. When it wrapped its limbs around his face, he struggled to break free.

Finally, with all his strength, Ethan ripped the monster from his back and catapulted it away from him.

Splat! The blob flattened into a starlike shape against the wall.

Ethan watched in horror as it peeled itself off the wall and flopped to the ground. It lay still for a moment, and then it began to squeal and squirm. The being popped back up to its feet and fluffed itself back into its blobby shape—good as new.

"Whaaat?" Ethan cried. Now that he could see it, the little blue guy didn't look quite so scary. "That is so weird," murmured Ethan, "but also . . . kinda cool."

The creature dusted itself off and seemed to be checking out its own limbs, making sure everything was intact. It chortled and chirped, shaking its rear.

"Hey," said Ethan. As he took a step forward, the blobby thing took a step back. "Hey, buddy. Hey, it's okay. It's okay—I'm friendly. See?" He knelt down to its height. "I'm a friend. See? We're all friends."

Ethan reached out his hand. The blob extended one of its many limbs toward Ethan's hand. Then . . . *smack!* It slapped Ethan's hand.

"Ahhh!" Ethan cried. "Ow!" He shook his hand in pain.

The critter strutted away with attitude, as if to say, "Serves you right."

"Okay. Yeah," said Ethan, taking a step back, "I guess I deserve that. I did splat you into a wall."

The strange being disappeared into a corner of the dark cave and emerged with something it had dropped—Searcher's bandanna.

Ethan recognized it immediately. "Hey, that's my dad's! Where'd you get that?"

The blob swung the bandanna side to side, as if playing a game of keep-away.

"Can you bring me to him?" asked Ethan. He made the *walking* gesture with his fingers, hoping the alien would understand.

And it did. As it scampered toward the cave's exit, Ethan fell in step behind it. "I'm so lucky I ran into you," said Ethan, hurrying to keep up. "Seriously, you don't know what I've been through. By the way, you're not dangerous, right? I mean, you don't look dangerous."

But as he followed the blue creature through the dark cave, Ethan couldn't be *entirely* sure. . . .

Jaeger speed walked through a field of long fleshy stems that grew out of the ground like tall grass.

Whoosh! He blasted his flamethrower, carving out a walking path for Searcher and Legend to follow. "The quickest route to your flying machine is through that valley up ahead," said Jaeger.

Searcher hustled to keep up with his father. "Okay, I have so many questions," he said. He turned as Legend playfully rolled down the hill toward the weird, tree-filled landscape before them. "Like, for one, what is this place?"

"A strange world where everything's alive and most things want to eat ya," Jaeger answered.

Just then, Searcher heard heavy footsteps and looked up as a large dinosaur-like creature with long spindly legs stopped over him. He cowered. "Uh . . . you mean like this thing?" he asked.

Jaeger looked up casually. "Naw, it's harmless."

Suddenly, dozens of nubby orb beings jumped off the back of the giant animal.

"And these things?" Searcher asked, covering his head with his arms as they rained down around him.

Jaeger chuckled and picked up a nubbin. "Funny little goobers, aren't they?" He tossed it to the side, and Legend pounced after it. "Every time I blaze a trail, they unblaze it."

As if on cue, the nubbins spilled onto the pathway Jaeger had cleared with his flamethrower. As the creatures were absorbed into the ground, new grass sprouted from the earth. The nubbins seemed to be *healing* the grassy field. Legend nosed the ground in confusion.

"Riiight," Searcher said, baffled by this strange place. "Um, so how did you even end up down here?" he asked.

"Through ingenuity and sheer tenacity," Jaeger boasted. He recalled it all clearly, beginning with a very long and arduous hike over the mountains. "After months of battling the elements, I figured there was no way anyone could ever survive walking over those cold, deadly peaks. So I went searching for a new path."

Jaeger pictured the moment years ago when he had stepped into a cave and the ground gave way beneath his feet. "And I found this place," he continued. "And it occurred to me: Instead of going over those mountains, I'll go *under* them—even if I had to fight every monster down here. Reapers and all!" He squared his shoulders, remembering his first battle with same type of tentacled beast that had gone after Searcher.

"Nothing was gonna stop Jaeger Clade from fulfilling his destiny!" he declared. "That is, until I came upon . . . *the Burning Sea*." He said the words reverently, picturing the sizzling acid that had almost consumed him. "A place where the cliffs are alive and the waters will dissolve the flesh off your bones."

Jaeger faced Searcher. "But *now,* with that flying ship of yours, we got a way to fly right over it and on to the other side of the mountains!"

"Wait," said Searcher, trying to make sense of his father's words. "You've been stuck in this underground nightmare for the past twenty-five years, and all you can think about are those mountains?"

"Oh, I'm not stuck down here," Jaeger casually replied.

"What?" Searcher said, pausing in his tracks. "You mean you could have come home whenever you wanted?"

"There is no going home until I finish my mission," Jaeger declared. "You should know that. You're an explorer!"

"Whoa, whoa, whoa there," said Searcher, holding up his hands. "I am not an explorer. I am a farmer."

Jaeger's face contorted. "A farmer?!" he spat. "Your mom has a lot of explaining to do."

Searcher hesitated. "She's gone, Dad."

Jaeger froze. "Penelope's . . . dead?" he whispered.

"Dead?" Searcher squawked. "No, she's not dead! She's sixty and works out five days a week. I said she was *gone*. As in, moved on. With Sheldon."

Jaeger's brow furrowed.

"Twenty-five years, Dad," Searcher said, glowering, too. "We thought you were dead for *twenty-five* years. What did you think was gonna happen?"

Jaeger took a deep breath. In one swift angry movement, he raced toward the cliff ahead and leaped right over its edge.

"Whoa! What the—" Searcher raced forward, too. He stopped just short of the cliff and peered down.

There was Jaeger, clinging fearlessly to the cliff's face by his fingertips. "I AM GONNA KILL SHELDON!" he roared.

"What?" called Searcher.

"I've always hated him!" Jaeger raged as he scaled expertly down the cliff's face.

Searcher threw out his hands. "You've never met him," he said.

"I hate his name," Jaeger said, jumping from one narrow ledge to the next. "And I'll probably hate his face." He continued free-climbing down the rocks, muttering all the way.

Legend bounded up to Searcher's side and watched as Jaeger continued to rage on the side of the cliff.

"I'd say he's taking this really well," Searcher said with a chuckle.

But Legend didn't want to be left behind. He hurtled his own three-legged self over the cliff and scampered after Jaeger.

"Holy—" Searcher cried. He had no choice now but to follow.

Chapter Seven

Near the fallen *Venture,* a pink blobby creature crept toward a piece of airship debris. It poked at it. When the hunk of metal shifted, the creature startled. It raced off and waved its limbs at something in the distance.

Two Reapers rolled forward, opened their horrific mouths, and shot forth their tentacle-like tongues. They fought over the tasty snack. With a crunch, a swallow, and a burp, the piece of the *Venture* was gone.

The little pink creature gave a satisfied nod and began leading the Reapers back to their hive.

On a nearby hill, Ethan's blue blobby companion waved its arms at the retreating Reapers. It jumped up and down as if to say, "Wait! C'mere! I found something for you, too!"

But the Reapers didn't see. When they rolled away, the little blue blob slumped in defeat.

Meanwhile, Ethan was too busy chatting and marveling at the strange landscape to notice the Reapers. "This place is so crazy," he was saying. "Who knew that this was all down here? I mean, *you* knew this was down here because you're from here. But it's not like this up top. These colors? These colors are so trippy. And these trees! Ah, even the trees are cool!" As he reached out to hug a strange tree, its trunk inflated and deflated like a balloon. Ethan laughed and pulled away. "Why is it doing that, Splat?"

The blue blob chattered something in response.

"Oh, by the way," said Ethan, hurrying toward it. "Do you mind if I call you Splat? I just came up with it. You just kind of give me Splat vibes. So I just thought—"

Before Ethan could say more, the creature turned its back and launched off the hill, somersaulting down the rocks.

"Wait, are you offended?" Ethan called after it. "I can't tell. You know what? I'll just follow you."

Meridian tightened the final bolt of a new side panel on the *Venture*. She knocked on it to check its stability. When it stayed firmly in place, she nodded with satisfaction. "It's not pretty, but it'll get us back airborne," she told Callisto.

"I gotta say, Meridian," Callisto said, "for a crop duster, you are one gutsy pilot."

Meridian reddened at the compliment. "Well, the three things I love most are my family, my farm, and flying," she replied. "If that last thing can protect the other two, I'd fly through fire."

Caspian approached. "Uh, Mrs. Clade—" he started to say.

"Yeah, what's up?" asked Meridian, still admiring her handiwork.

"Remember how I was given the crucial responsibility of watching your son?" he asked.

Meridian smiled knowingly and started gathering her tools. "Is he giving you trouble? You can send him back to me. I'll put him to work," she said, pointing to the battered airship.

"I would *love* to do that, except . . ." Caspian shrugged sheepishly. "I don't know where he is."

Meridian spun around with alarm. "What?!"

Jaeger and Searcher had reached a tricky part of the terrain. As Jaeger swiftly leaped from ledge to ledge, Searcher lagged behind, grunting as he hoisted himself up the steep rock face.

"Searcher!" Jaeger called. He was dangling from the cliff with ease. "You call that climbing?"

"I'm a forty-year-old man that farms," said Searcher as he cautiously worked his way higher. "Climbing isn't really part of my day-to-day."

"So . . . you just forgot"—Jaeger swung himself over the ledge of the rock wall—"everything I taught you?"

"No," said Searcher, struggling to pull himself up. "Just the pointless explorer stuff. So yeah, everything."

Jaeger reached out a hand and yanked Searcher to the top. "Scoff all you want," he said. "But when I get past those mountains, I'll return to Avalonia a hero." He stomped the ground to make sure it was solid, causing a huge glob of goo to fall from the ceiling. It plopped onto Searcher, burying him in muck.

Jaeger didn't seem to notice as he carried on. "Bet they even give me a statue in the town square."

"You already have a statue," Searcher mumbled, wiping the goo from his face with both hands.

Jaeger whirled around. "I do?"

"Yeah, and it's right beside mine," said Searcher, saying that last part loud and clear.

Before Searcher could say another word, he was enveloped in soft bristles that shot down from above. A moment later, the bristles retreated, and Searcher, still startled, found himself wiped clean of the goo. A strange animal galloped away from him across the ceiling, a tuft of silky hair fluttering where its head should be.

Jaeger paid no mind to Searcher as he plopped down on a rock next to Legend. "*You* have a statue?" he chuckled. "What, do they just give statues to everybody these days?"

"No, Dad," said Searcher, "I discovered Pando. You know, the thing I'm actually down here to save, the discovery that actually changed the world and transformed Avalonia into the utopia that it is today. And—not that it matters—but my statue's taller."

Jaeger stood and took off again, hopping over a path of stones. "So much for the whole humble farmer bit, huh?" he called. "Maybe you're more like me than you wanna admit."

Searcher followed, until the stone he was balancing on stood up on four legs and scampered away. "I'm *nothing* like you," he insisted.

"Uh-huh," said Jaeger, patting Legend on the head. "Just keep telling yourself that."

The two climbed another rocky formation. Searcher gritted his teeth as he made it over the ridge. "Whatever," he said. "I created a *real* legacy—"

He paused, reaching his foot down to feel for a ledge to step onto. But when he found one, the ground moved beneath him—carrying him with it.

"What? Whoa, whoa!" he shouted. Searcher looked down. He wasn't standing on a ledge anymore. And he wasn't standing on a four-legged scampering rock, either. He was perched precariously on a clear, enormous sluglike creature. "Whoa. Hey there," he said to the creature. He glanced at his father. "Is this thing dangerous?"

Jaeger shrugged. "Maybe." He grabbed a strange bug that was flying by, stuffed it in his mouth, and crunched with satisfaction.

Suddenly, Searcher's feet began to sink. "Ahhh!" he cried as he was absorbed by the transparent slug creature. Legend barked and leaped onto the creature before sinking into it alongside Searcher.

As Searcher struggled to get out, Jaeger chuckled. Then he spotted something on the ground. "Hold it," he said, crouching next to a card that read PRIMAL OUTPOST.

"There's someone else out here," he said to himself.

Searcher tried to call to Jaeger from inside the belly of the see-through slug. "That's Ethan's!" he cried. "That's Ethan's!" But his voice sounded muffled.

"What?" asked Jaeger, struggling to understand. Finally, he reached into the creature's stomach and pulled Searcher and Legend out.

"I . . . said . . . ," cried Searcher, gasping for air, "that's . . . Ethan's!"

"Who's Ethan?" Jaeger asked.

Searcher rose to his feet and took the playing card from his father. "My son!"

"Your son?" Jaeger said, his eyes wide. "Jaeger Clade . . . is a grandpa?"

"I guess . . . technically . . . yes," said Searcher.

Jaeger considered this for a moment before he noticed footprints trailing away from where they stood.

"Well, he's not alone," said Jaeger, observing a second set of prints that were definitely *not* human.

Searcher's and Jaeger's eyes followed the prints toward the horizon, where a purplish mass hovered above the ground. Jaeger knew all too well what lived in that hive. Which meant Ethan was in trouble.

Chapter Eight

*T*he little blue creature that Ethan had named Splat led him to the base of that very same hive. Splat signaled for Ethan to stand still.

Ethan glanced up with curiosity at the dark bulbous mass. "Whoa," he said, "what is this thing?"

Splat didn't answer. Instead, the creature leaped up to the hive and began scaling its side.

Ethan called after Splat. "Hey, we're still looking for my dad, right?"

Splat nodded and pointed again, as if reminding Ethan to stay right where he was.

Then Splat hurried up the hive toward two enormous Reapers who were sleeping. Splat poked them awake and gestured down toward Ethan. Except . . . Ethan had wandered away!

Splat signaled to the Reapers to wait a moment. Then the little blue blob plopped back down to the ground and went looking for its missing victim.

Just a few yards away, Ethan was rifling through some wreckage from the *Venture*. He had discovered a crate of Pando and was loading up his backpack with pods.

Splat crept up behind Ethan and tapped its foot impatiently.

"Yeah, yeah, I know, I know," said Ethan. "But this Pando fell off the *Venture*. And we don't waste pods. So I'm just going to grab it really quick, okay?"

Splat squealed in irritation. The Reapers were waiting! Splat yanked on Ethan's arm and tried to pull him away.

"Hang on, hang on!" Ethan protested. "Really quick. Just lemme grab the rest of these."

Splat pulled a pod right out of Ethan's hand, trying to shut this operation down.

Zap! The Pando shocked Splat, sending convulsions through the creature's entire body. *Zap! Zap! Zap!* Splat shrieked in pain.

"Splat?" cried Ethan. "Splat!"

Splat tried flinging the pod away, but it stuck to its limb as if glued on. Ethan pried the Pando out of Splat's grip. As Splat fell and crept away, Ethan could see the painful burn the Pando had left behind. Splat whined in fear and pain.

"Here, it's okay," said Ethan soothingly, stretching out his hand. "I can help you with that."

Ethan searched for anything he could use to help Splat. He grabbed his dad's bandanna and a bottle of water to wet the cloth. Then he slowly approached Splat. "Let me see," said Ethan gently.

Splat squealed, unsure.

"You can trust me," said Ethan, offering his open palm.

Finally, a tentative Splat held out its injured limb.

As Ethan wrapped the cool, wet bandanna tenderly over the burn, Splat turned away and whimpered. "It's okay. It's okay," Ethan repeated, dabbing the wound. Finally, Splat stopped crying. The little creature's body eased.

Ethan smiled as he tied the bandanna into a makeshift bandage. "There you go," he said. "Good as new."

Splat stood up, looking much happier—until something roared from nearby. Splat had summoned the Reapers. And now they were coming. . . .

"He's with a *what*?" cried Searcher.

He, Jaeger, and Legend were racing toward Ethan on the head of the sluglike creature—the one that had absorbed Searcher whole. Somehow, Jaeger knew how to ride it. He also knew that Ethan was in serious trouble.

"A scout for the Reapers," hollered Jaeger. He had recognized the footprints that ran alongside Ethan's. He'd encountered many blobs like Splat before. "They only got one job—to lure you to your death."

"What?" Searcher cried out again. "Can this thing move faster?"

"Hiyah!" Jaeger hollered, urging the beast forward.

As the creature's many legs sped up, they raced toward the dark hive on the horizon.

But the Reapers were already there.

As five fearsome beasts rolled toward Ethan, he gave a weak wave. "Hi, I'm Ethan," he said, stepping backward. "I thought Splat here was bringing me to my dad. Maybe I was wrong. I don't see my dad anywhere. . . ."

Splat waved its limbs wildly, trying to call off the Reapers. Ethan was a *friendly* human, Splat wanted to say. A helpful human. But it was too late. A Reaper smacked Splat aside and lunged for Ethan.

"I'll just be on my way!" Ethan cried, leaping out of the Reaper's path.

But he couldn't go forward. And he couldn't go backward. Reapers had rolled in, blocking his path on all sides.

The giant slug reached the hive just in time. When Jaeger caught sight of Ethan, he leaped off the slug and landed beside his grandson. Their eyes met briefly, and Jaeger offered a reassuring wink before he fired up his flamethrower and blasted the tentacles of the nearest Reaper.

"Whoa," Ethan whispered, awestruck by the man courageously fighting back the monsters.

Searcher jumped to the ground beside him. "Ethan!" he cried, throwing out his arms to protect his son from the Reapers' darting tentacles.

"Dad!" Ethan shouted, relieved to see him.

"Stay behind me," ordered Jaeger. He aimed his flamethrower and roasted another beast.

"Who's he?" Ethan pointed at the burly gray-haired man.

"Ethan, meet your grandpa," said Searcher.

Ethan's eyes widened. "That's Jaeger Clade?"

"The one and only!" Jaeger called over his shoulder. Then he glanced up and spotted a way out. A red stream of fishlike creatures flowed overhead.

"Follow me!" Jaeger ordered. He blasted a path through the Reapers with his flamethrower. Beasts rolled right and left, away from the flickering flames.

Ethan and Searcher raced ahead. But when they reached the edge of a cliff, the Reapers were still coming. "Now what?" Searcher cried, staring at the red stream that flowed past the cliff.

"Jump!" ordered Jaeger.

But Jaeger didn't wait for Searcher and Ethan to

jump. He pushed them both from behind. Legend followed dutifully, leaping eagerly off the edge of the cliff.

"Ahhhhhhhhhh!" they wailed as they plunged toward the crimson torrent.

They landed safely atop the river of swimming creatures, which carried them forward in a rushing stream.

"Whoa!" said Ethan in amazement as he knelt on the backs of the creatures. "What are these things?"

"Our ticket outta here," Jaeger called. He hopped up and began running along the flowing red walkway.

Legend let out a happy *woof*, but Searcher hesitated. "They're not gonna eat us, right?" he asked.

"No," said Jaeger. "But *they* will!" He pointed backward.

"What?"

Reapers were still chasing them!

"Just run!" Jaeger hollered.

Searcher sprinted as fast as he could. But when he tripped, he fell face-first into the wriggling red stream of creatures. He struggled to swim forward, nearly plunging out of the torrent to the depths below. And the Reapers were right behind him.

"Dad!" Ethan cried as a Reaper latched on to Searcher's foot with its long tentacle.

Jaeger bounded back toward Searcher and yanked

on his hand. "Come on, Searcher," he said impatiently. "Stop embarrassing me out here! Move!" He pulled Searcher free and then raised his flamethrower to blast the encroaching Reapers.

As Jaeger held the Reapers back, Searcher ran for his life along the red trail, racing toward Ethan and Legend.

"He's awesome!" said Ethan as Searcher caught up to him.

"He is *not* awesome," Searcher argued.

"He just saved my life!" Ethan exclaimed.

"Ya know, I was part of that rescue, too," Searcher grumbled.

"He just saved *your* life," Ethan pointed out.

"Ya ain't seen nothing yet, kid!" Jaeger boasted as he ran up alongside them. He laughed and then aimed his flamethrower at the red stream behind them. As he blew a hole in the stream, Reapers plummeted into the depths.

But the red fishlike creatures beneath Searcher's and Ethan's feet began to fall away, too. Searcher watched his son slide right off the trail. "No, Ethan!"

As Ethan sailed downward, belly first and screaming, Splat hitched a ride on a wayward fishy creature and snatched Ethan's foot—just in time.

"Splat!" cried Ethan as his little blue friend delivered him safely back to Searcher. "Thanks, buddy."

"Are you okay?" asked Searcher.

Splat, who was now riding on Ethan's back, gave the A-OK signal.

"I'm talking to my *son*," Searcher said.

"I'm fine, Dad," Ethan replied.

Searcher, however, was *not* fine. He was done with Jaeger's antics, which had put Ethan in danger. As Jaeger pumped his arms and raced past them, Searcher said, "Can you not show off while we're running for our lives?"

"Calm down," said Jaeger. "The kid's all right."

Searcher huffed. "How are *you* my dad?"

"Oh, you wanna have that conversation?" said Jaeger. "Well, when two people love each other—"

Searcher clamped his hands over his ears. "Stop talking. Stop talking. Stop talking. . . ."

Jaeger chanced another glance over his shoulder. The Reapers were still coming. "Time for a barbecue," he declared. He aimed his flamethrower at the mass of Reapers and pulled the trigger.

A small *poof* of smoke popped out of the end. The flamethrower needed fuel.

"That ain't good!" Jaeger groaned.

Just then, two skiffs zoomed into view. Callisto landed her vehicle on the red highway behind Jaeger—blocking the Reapers. Meridian skidded her skiff to a stop in front of her family.

"Get on!" Meridian shouted. Legend leaped onto the skiff, beside Meridian, sharing the driver's seat.

"Meridian!" cried Searcher, never happier to see his wife.

"Mom!" yelled Ethan.

Meridian shot her son a stern look. "Oh, no, no, no, no. . . . Don't you *mom* me," she said. "Once we're home, your butt is grounded for life!"

Jaeger gave a grunt of approval as he hopped on the skiff, beside Searcher. "Oh, I like her," he said, nodding toward Meridian.

"Who's he?" Meridian asked Searcher.

"My dad," he said with a sigh.

"What?" squawked Meridian.

But there wasn't time for introductions. "Hurry up!" called Callisto as the Reapers scrambled closer, their tentacles reaching for the group. "Go, go, go!"

Meridian hit the throttle and kept pace with Callisto. But as they barreled ahead, they found themselves heading straight toward a cluster of purple hives. Scads of Reapers scuttled down from the hives like spiders.

"Uh, wall of monsters!" cried Searcher. "Wall of monsters!"

"Don't worry," said Callisto. "I got this." She gunned her engine, and as her skiff shot forward, she flipped off the back end—landing on Meridian's skiff.

Callisto's skiff rocketed toward the Reapers. They dodged the hurtling vehicle easily. The skiff whizzed past the beasts and hit the hive in a fiery explosion— but the monsters kept coming.

"Okay," said Callisto. "So they're smarter than they look."

"I coulda told you that," Jaeger teased.

Callisto took him in for the first time. "Jaeger Clade?" she said in disbelief.

"The one and—" Jaeger started to say.

"We know!" said Searcher, shutting him down. How could Jaeger boast at a time like this? The Reapers were closing in, and now the skiff was surrounded.

Meridian gunned the throttle, but the skiff had become lodged between the swimming creatures. "Uh, guys," she cried as the Reapers rolled toward them. "We're stuck!"

Splat suddenly had an idea. The little blue blob pointed at the Pando pods in Ethan's pack.

"Great idea, Splat!" said Ethan. He pulled his pack off his back.

"Splat? Its name is Splat?" asked Searcher.

Ethan didn't have time to explain. He opened his backpack and flung the Pando pods forward and backward, straight into the paths of the Reapers. The pods lit up the monsters like fireworks.

Meridian spotted an escape route ahead of them. Another red stream intersected the first, heading to the left.

"Callisto, give us a push!" Meridian shouted.

Callisto hopped out. "I'm on it!" She kicked with the toe of her boot to nudge the squirmy beings aside, dislodging the skiff. Then she climbed back on.

"Hang on, everybody!" shouted Meridian. She skillfully rocketed away from the Reapers, flying the relieved group to safety.

Chapter Nine

Securely inside the hanger bay of the *Venture,* the Clades, Callisto, and Splat climbed off the skiff.

Caspian came running and pulled Ethan in for a hug. "I'm so glad you're safe, little Ethan!" Caspian said as if they were old friends. "You had me so worried!"

Feeling the love, Splat threw its arms around Caspian and Ethan, giving a satisfied squeal.

Caspian gasped with delight when he saw Splat. "Aw, what is that? It's so cute!" he said, lifting the little blue blob into the air. Splat struggled to escape as Caspian hugged it like a teddy bear.

Meanwhile, Jaeger slapped a side panel of the *Venture.* "This'll do just fine," he said. "Other side of the mountains, here I come."

"Okay, that's not what we're here to do," Searcher reminded him.

"Right," said Jaeger, rolling his eyes. "Your silly little plant."

Searcher threw up his hands. "It's not a silly plant."

"Fine," Jaeger conceded. "Your boring plant."

"You know what I find boring?" Searcher asked.

"Your terrible comeback?" Jaeger answered.

Searcher rolled his eyes. "What? No. Ugh! *You!*"

"Clever," Jaeger teased.

Everyone looked on as the two Clades continued to argue.

Finally, Callisto stepped between the bickering men. "Okay, adult speaking here!" she announced. "Let me remind everybody: the mission is to get to Pando's heart. 'Cause as we can all see, we're on a clock." She pointed at the ceiling to demonstrate her point.

Searcher smirked at Jaeger, but when he looked up, he watched as a long strand of Pando root withered and crumbled to dust.

"But after we do that," Callisto told Jaeger, "there's nothing stopping us from continuing on to see what's on the other side. Sound like a fair deal?"

Jaeger nodded and offered Searcher a smirk of his own.

"Okay, then. It's settled," Callisto said, clapping both men on the shoulder.

Just then, Searcher noticed Ethan looking up at

his grandfather with the same awestruck expression he'd had while gazing at Jaeger's statue.

"Hey, buddy," Searcher said, getting Ethan's attention. "Wanna give me a hand? Let's see if we can get a sample from that Pando root."

As Ethan followed his dad, Splat ran to Searcher's side and offered him the stolen bandanna, as if calling a truce.

"Uh, thanks," Searcher said.

Eager to move forward with the mission, Callisto gestured to the cockpit. "Meridian, care to do the honors?"

Meridian looked around at her family and then grinned. She was ready to take the wheel.

Meridian confidently slid into the pilot's seat. "All right, *Venture*," she said. "I guess this makes us official. Just don't make me look bad in front of my family."

With Meridian at the helm, the *Venture* whirred to life and rose high above the thicket of glowing trees. Onward they flew, over cliffs and through forests, soaring deeper into the strange world.

As they reached a tangled mass of Pando roots growing across the ceiling, Searcher stood atop a ladder on the airship's deck and examined the roots. He reached his Pando picker up to trim off a thin tendril of healthy Pando root. Ethan waited below the ladder with a bucket, prepared to catch the root sample when it fell. But as Searcher's Pando picker made contact with the root's insides, *zap!* It sent a quick shock through his body, knocking him off his feet.

Searcher sat on the deck in a daze, his hair standing straight up. When Legend bounded over to lick his face, Ethan couldn't help but laugh.

When Searcher had recovered, they brought the root sample to the ship's lab, where a crew member with hexagonally framed glasses studied the Pando through a microscope. Searcher took a turn looking through the scope and marveled as the Pando root cells glowed and sparked with energy. But when they compared that sample to one from a rotten Pando pod, they couldn't find any sign of a pest that might be making Pando sick.

Soon, there was commotion outside the lab.

"Whoa!" cried a crew member. "It's Jaeger Classic!"

"The one and only!" quipped Jaeger, who had just stepped out of the cabin looking like a new man. His face was clean-shaven except for his signature moustache. Now he looked more like the father Searcher had once known. The hero of Avalonia was back, and everyone wanted his autograph—even Callisto.

Searcher didn't see what the big deal was, but

Ethan stared in awe at his grandfather, the legendary explorer he had always dreamed of meeting.

Searcher couldn't help but worry about Ethan's new obsession with Jaeger. He may even have felt a little jealous. But he stayed quiet and let Ethan have his moment.

As the *Venture* continued on its journey, Ethan explored the ship with Splat and Legend. They wandered along the catwalks, taking in the strange sights and unusual creatures they passed.

There were some now! Legend barked at fluffy blossom-like beings that floated around the ship's deck. One of the creatures landed momentarily in Ethan's open palms before lifting off again to join its friends. Then a group of the bugs attached themselves to Legend's rump and carried him into the air. Ethan chased after him, holding on to Splat's elastic legs as the blue blob stretched as far as it could to grab Legend out of the sky and bring him back to the safety of the deck.

Soon the ship entered a new landscape of rocky amber land formations. Enormous gentle creatures with quills along their curved spines and long barbed tails floated alongside the ship. Ethan gasped and took a step backward. Were these beasts friends or foes? Splat reached out to one and touched its smooth back, showing Ethan that it was friendly. So Ethan summoned his courage and touched it, too. As he did, light rays shimmered throughout the visitor's body.

Ethan gazed at the glowing creature in awe—until his grandfather stepped onto the catwalk.

"Hey, get outta here!" Jaeger hollered, waving the beautiful creature away. "C'mon, git! Git! Git! Shoo!"

When the creature retreated, Jaeger looked down at Ethan proudly, as if he'd just saved his grandson's life.

"Seemed pretty harmless to me," said Ethan. "But you do you."

"Eh, better safe than sorry." Jaeger replied. He leaned against the rail and turned toward Ethan. "So, you're my grandson, huh?"

"That's the rumor," said Ethan.

"Well, tell me about yourself, Ethan," said Jaeger. "What are you into? Fighting? Hunting? Any sweet-hearts waiting for ya back home?"

Ethan's cheeks burned with embarrassment, and he looked away.

"Ah, there it is," Jaeger teased. "Who is it?"

"It's no one," said Ethan at first. Then he grinned, and it all came spilling out. "Diazo. His name is Diazo."

"Diazo, huh?" said Jaeger with a smile.

"I really like him a lot," Ethan went on. "I just don't know how to tell him because . . . I just get so *this.* . . . I always get so *this!*" He gestured at his flushed face.

"Hey!" said Jaeger, raising his hands. "Let your grandpa give you some solid advice. If you really, really want to impress this fella, this is what you do."

Ethan leaned in, eager to hear.

Jaeger grabbed Splat and then hopped up on the deck rail. "You get him into a dangerous situation," Jaeger explained, balancing on one leg as if he might fall. "Like, maybe one in which he almost dies." As Jaeger stepped off the rail, Splat squealed.

Ethan ran to the rail and saw Jaeger clinging to the side of the ship—and Splat clinging to Jaeger. "And then you save him from it!" Jaeger called, tossing Splat up to the safety of Ethan's arms. "Bonus points if it includes bandits, alligators, and/or spectacular explosions."

Jaeger climbed back on deck and fired off his flamethrower, demonstrating the "explosions" part.

Ethan cocked his head. "Yeah, all that sounds like a really toxic way to start a relationship," he said. From his shoulder, Splat chirped in agreement. "Not to mention crazy dangerous," Ethan added.

Jaeger put a hand on his hip and laughed.

"Dangerous? You're a Clade. We love danger." He handed Ethan his flamethrower. "Go ahead, give it a try."

"Uh, really?" said Ethan. He reached for the weapon just as Searcher arrived, having run to the deck after seeing the blast of fire from Jaeger's flamethrower.

Searcher watched in horror as Ethan assumed a Jaeger Clade stance, pointing the flamethrower at some imaginary beast and blowing it away. For just a moment, Searcher actually saw Ethan as a miniature Jaeger Clade—moustache and all.

Searcher watched Jaeger give Ethan a hearty slap on the back. "That's a Clade boy right there!"

"Pando Schmando," Searcher imagined Ethan saying before giving Jaeger a high five.

Searcher marched forward, waving his Pando picker. "Hey, Dad," he called to Jaeger, trying to sound casual. "Um, I really appreciate you bonding with Ethan here, but maybe a flamethrower isn't his thing."

Jaeger responded in an equally polite tone. "I appreciate that you think that, but maybe Ethan doesn't know *his thing* unless he tries. So go ahead, kiddo." He nodded at Ethan, urging him to fire the flamethrower again.

Searcher laughed, which sounded more like a squawk. "Well, I appreciate your enthusiasm, but

Ethan already has a *thing,* and that's a Pando picker. And he's really good with it." He shoved the Pando picker into Ethan's hands.

Jaeger feigned a smile. "I appreciate your appreciation, but maybe we let the kid decide."

Ethan glanced from his father to his grandfather. Was it time to break up this fight?

"Ah, well I appreciate your appreciation," said Searcher, his voice tight, "but maybe you appreciate *me* a little bit more and respect my wishes, please."

Ethan groaned.

"And maybe you should step out of my air," Jaeger barked back.

Yep, it was time for Ethan to break this up—definitely. He held up the Pando picker and the flamethrower between the bickering men. *"Or . . . ,"* Ethan suggested, "maybe we lower the temperature a little bit."

"Oh-kay," said Jaeger slowly. "What do you have in mind?"

Ethan pulled a deck of cards from his pocket. "A little Primal Outpost?" he proposed with a grin.

Chapter Ten

Jaeger, Searcher, Ethan, and Splat were deep into gameplay, their Primal Outpost cards spread out across a deck table.

"Can someone trade me a weapon?" asked Jaeger, studying his cards. "All I got is dirt and gardening tools."

"I have masonry stones," Searcher offered.

Jaeger considered this. "Chucking stones could be effective," he decided.

"So . . . that's not what masonry stones are for," Ethan gently noted.

"He's right," Jaeger said thoughtfully. "I need crossbows." He turned to Splat, who was also playing. "You got any crossbows?"

When Jaeger tried to peek at Splat's cards, Splat slapped his hand away. Then the creature reached out a long limb and grabbed a bunch of Searcher's cards.

"Hey, Splat just stole my cards!" Searcher cried. He leaned across the table to take his cards back, but Splat slapped his hand, too.

"Ya get anything good?" Jaeger asked, leaning over again to peek at Splat's cards.

But the last grain of sand had just fallen in the Primal Outpost hourglass. "Time's up!" Ethan announced. "Trading period has ended."

"Aha—a crossbow!" cried Jaeger as he lifted Splat off the ground. Several cards were stuck to Splat's belly, including one with a crossbow. "I knew you were holding out on me!"

"Okay!" said Ethan, trying to take back control. "Event card time." He shuffled the cards and drew one. "Are you ready to deal with"—he flipped over the card dramatically—"a demon spider?"

"Kill it!" Jaeger cried, smashing his meaty palm on top of the card.

"Uh-uh, the point is not to kill it," Ethan said, peeling Jaeger's hand off the card. "I know *demon spider* sounds scary, but—"

"Oh yeah, that thing will devour our crops for sure," said Searcher.

Jaeger glared at him. "*That's* what you're worried about?"

Ethan massaged his temples as he explained

the game one more time, trying his best to stay calm. "The objective of Primal Outpost is to live *harmoniously* with your environment."

"I throw masonry stones at it!" Searcher decided, slapping down his card.

"And I shoot it with my brand-new crossbow," declared Jaeger, presenting the card he had just stolen from Splat.

Ethan threw up his hands in defeat. "Okay, fine. It's dead," he said. "See? You killed it."

"That's what I'm talking about!" boasted Jaeger. He offered Searcher a fist bump, which Searcher returned with an awkward high five. So Jaeger offered a high five, which Searcher fist-bumped.

"Oh, but wait . . . ," Ethan said in a low, ominous voice. "The demon spider was the only thing keeping the murder locusts from destroying all your resources. Congrats, you're dead!" He snatched away their cards with a satisfied sweep of his hands.

Splat squawked in frustration.

"I agree with that snot bubble here," said Jaeger. "What?"

"Wait, the demon spider wasn't the bad guy?" asked Searcher, raising an eyebrow.

"For the twenty-seventh time," said Ethan, "there *are* no bad guys. The objective isn't to kill or destroy monsters. You're just supposed to build a working civilization utilizing the environment around you."

Jaeger and Searcher nodded. "Uh-huh," they said. "Uh-huh."

Then Jaeger gave Ethan a blank stare. "Yeah, I don't get this game."

"Me neither," said Searcher.

"Oh, come on! It is *not* that complicated!" Ethan grabbed his head with his hands.

"Maybe I'll just farm Pando," Searcher suggested.

"Pando's not part of the game," said Ethan through clenched teeth.

"Can we conquer the monsters and use them as weapons?" asked Jaeger.

"Monsters. Aren't. Weapons," said Ethan.

Even Splat seemed to disagree with Ethan now, chattering some argument of its own.

"What?" said Ethan, as if he understood every word. "No!"

"Check out my new weapon," Jaeger announced, reaching for a new card from the deck.

"If he gets a monster, I get Pando," Searcher whined.

"No monster. No Pando!" cried Ethan.

"And no bad guys? What kind of game has no bad guys?" asked Searcher.

"That's just poor storytelling," Jaeger added.

Ethan curled his fingers into fists. "Okay, you know what?" he cried, stepping away from the table. "You want bad guys? Fine. You two are the bad guys! Because you *both* are annoying *me*." With that, he stormed off the deck.

An indignant Splat did exactly the same, tossing up its cards, storming out behind Ethan, and slamming the door.

As Searcher watched them go, he tried to laugh. "Teenagers, right?" he said, nudging his father.

But Jaeger was still fixated on the game. There was only one opponent left to conquer. So with one swift movement, he reached out and knocked over Searcher's game piece.

"I win," he announced with a satisfied smirk.

Later, in the cockpit, Jaeger leaned over Meridian's shoulder, staring at what lay ahead.

The *Venture* was approaching a sizzling body of acid inside a strange cavern. Green balloon creatures floated above the bubbling brew, as if afraid to touch its surface. Every now and then, the cavern walls undulated, squeezing in and out and sending acid shooting up the walls.

"The Burning Sea," said Jaeger gravely. "The one

obstacle that stands between Jaeger Clade and his destiny."

Meridian nudged him away. "Can you go be dramatic somewhere else?"

Searcher pulled out his binoculars. "It looks like the roots continue across the ceiling to the other side, where they seem relatively healthy," he told Callisto. "This place may be bad, but it's not our bad guy."

"Okay," said Callisto. "There must be a way around it."

"There ain't no way . . . but through," Jaeger announced in a gruff voice.

"Relax, Captain Dramatic," Meridian said. "Mama's got this. . . ." She flipped a series of switches and eased the *Venture* forward. As she carefully maneuvered the ship this way and that, she took special note of the geysers that shot up from the boiling lake.

"See that?" she asked Ethan.

He leaned forward over her shoulder and studied the lake's surface. "Yeah, it always bubbles right before it erupts."

Meridian nodded, proud of Ethan's shrewd observation. "That's my baby," she said. She slowed the airship's advance to avoid a sudden spurt of acid.

As the lake continued to roil, the cavern slowly filled with a foggy gas.

Meridian squinted at the haze. "I need someone to be my eyes!" she called out.

Ethan planted himself at the window and watched the surface of the lake for signs of geysers. "Bear left! Bear right!" he shouted as geysers shot up around them. "Stop! Go! Slowly. Slower. Stop!"

Meridian followed his directions, making her way through the ever-changing maze.

"Mom, we're almost there!" Ethan said, just making out a cavern exit on the edge of the lake just ahead. That's when he noticed that all the green balloon creatures had turned toward them and were now approaching the *Venture*. "Huh," said Ethan. "What are those things?"

In a rush, the balloon beings swarmed the airship. *Fffft! Fffft!* They clung to the windshield, making pooting noises as they used the *Venture* as a life raft.

"What are these little poot pickles doing?" Meridian cried. "Get off!"

As she flipped on the wipers to clear the windshield, she saw a tidal wave of acid rolling straight toward the *Venture*.

"Hold on to your barf bags," she shouted as she turned the steering wheel hard to the left. The airship veered sideways, barely escaping the surge. Then Meridian spotted an escape ahead: a small opening in the cavern, surrounded by spurting acid. As waves

Welcome to **Avalonia**, a humble but happy town surrounded by a ring of impassable mountains. Despite their rocky confines, the people of Avalonia have found a way to thrive, thanks to Pando, a plant that buzzes with energy.

When the Pando crops begin to fail, the leader of Avalonia organizes an expedition to find out what is wrong. The crew follows the plants' roots underground and finds a *strange world* filled with even stranger creatures!

Searcher Clade

Searcher is considered a hero in Avalonia for discovering Pando, the plant that powers their modern city. A dedicated family man, Searcher wants nothing more than to create a legacy for his son, Ethan, who he hopes will become a Pando farmer, just like him.

Teenager **Ethan** dreams of exploring beyond the confines of mountain-bound Avalonia and the family farm. When Searcher leaves on the expedition, Ethan stows away on the ship, hoping to find the excitement he is missing.

Meridian Clade

For **Meridian**, the best things in life are her family, their farm, and flying the crop duster. When she joins the expedition, she uses her skills as a pilot to protect her family and help save the world!

Jaeger Clade

Boisterous and confident, **Jaeger** is a famous explorer who journeyed alone to conquer Avalonia's impassable mountains and never returned. Now, twenty-five years later, he reunites with his son, Searcher, in the strange underground world.

Callisto Mal

Once a member of Jaeger Clade's exploration team, **Callisto** is now the president of Avalonia. Her daring past and her dedication to Avalonia make her the perfect leader for the expedition.

Legend

A lovable companion to the Clade family, **Legend** has a tendency to charge straight into danger. This fearless pup loves adventures and is just as daring on three legs as a dog with four!

Splat

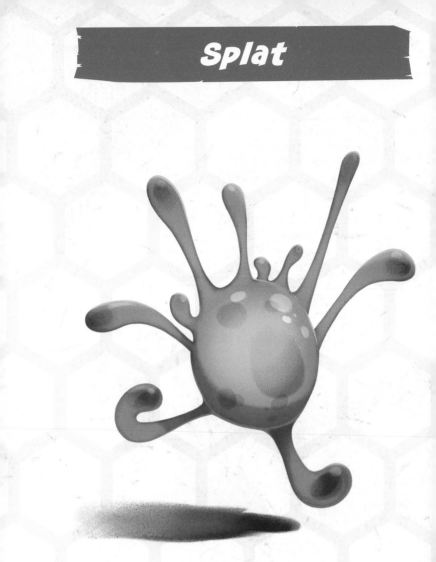

As a scout for the Reapers, *Splat* only has one job: to lure strangers to their death. But when Splat befriends Ethan, the little blue blob finds a new purpose in guiding the teenager around the mysterious underground land it calls home.

crashed around them, Meridian turned on the thrusters, sending the *Venture* rocketing toward the exit.

Seconds later, they emerged in a dark, peaceful place. Somehow, they had made it to the other side of the Burning Sea—alive.

There was a moment of silence while they all caught their breath. Then Ethan cheered. "Mom, you did it! That was so cool!"

"I knew you could do it," said Searcher, grinning at his wife.

"Well done, Meridian!" Callisto added.

"That's how you do it," Meridian said proudly.

Suddenly, the windshield shattered, ending the celebration. The Reapers had arrived. And they were angry.

Chapter Eleven

Jaeger leaped into action, storming out to the catwalk and using his flamethrower to hold the first Reaper back. He laughed fiendishly as the beast fell. But before long, another Reaper slithered forward, wrapping itself around Jaeger's body and throwing him to the deck. He aimed his flamethrower at the beast, but it grabbed the weapon from his hands.

"I got you, Jaeger," shouted Callisto. She lunged forward, pulled the flamethrower from the Reaper's clutches, and squeezed the trigger. *Whoosh!* Flames shot into the Reaper's gullet, driving it back.

"Ugh," she said as gave Jaeger his weapon, now dripping with Reaper goo. "I think this thing has seen better days."

"That's okay," shouted Searcher, appearing on the deck with a crate in his arms. "I've got a better weapon."

He slammed the crate down on the deck and pried

open the lid. Hundreds of pods were tucked inside. Searcher, Jaeger, and Callisto each grabbed a pod.

"Aim at center mass!" Jaeger ordered.

He and Callisto wound up and threw their pods at the same time. Both pods hit their mark—shocking the Reapers and pushing them back.

But when Searcher tossed his pod, it bounced weakly off the ground a few feet in front of him.

Callisto squinted in disbelief. "Wow," she said under her breath.

Jaeger didn't hide his disgust. "Who taught you how to throw?" he bellowed.

"Sheldon?" said Searcher with a shrug.

"Ugh," Jaeger groaned, agitated by the mention of Sheldon's name. He called to Callisto over his shoulder. "Keep us covered."

"On it!" she said, whipping another pod at the Reapers.

Then Jaeger stood before Searcher in a pitching stance. "All right. This is how you throw. Center your weight. Breathe in. Focus, and . . . ," Jaeger wound back his arm and released. "Follow through!"

The pod ricocheted between a few Reapers, electrocuting them all.

"See? It's all in the follow-through," Jaeger boasted. "All right, your turn."

Searcher picked up a pod and repeated his

father's instructions. "Center weight. Breathe. Focus, and . . . follow through!" He launched a pod and was surprised—and thrilled—when it took out a Reaper.

"There you go!" Jaeger exclaimed. "Now, take them out on the right!" He pointed.

Searcher grabbed a pod from the crate and hit another Reaper.

"Attaboy!" Jaeger cried. "Light 'em up!" He picked up some pods and joined Searcher. Together, they battled back the hoard of Reapers.

Then Searcher had a better idea. He pulled out his Pando picker and held it like a baseball bat. "Serve it up!" he cried to Jaeger. "C'mon, Pops!"

Jaeger pitched a bundle of Pando pods to Searcher. *Thwack!*

Searcher struck, sending the pods toward the Reapers at electrifying speed. "Yes!" he cried when the Pando exploded like fireworks, taking out a large flock of beasts. "Woo, hoo, hoo!"

"Aha!" said Jaeger.

As the *Venture* flew away from the remaining Reapers, Jaeger trash-talked the creatures. "You think you can take us, you squiggly armed night-mares? You ain't nothing against the Clades!"

Later, it was time to celebrate. Searcher brought a couple of bottles to the deck and offered one to Jaeger. "Not too bad for a farmer, right?" he said, hoping he had made his father proud during their battle with the Reapers.

Jaeger chuckled. "Yeah, not too bad at all."

They sipped from their bottles in silence. Then Jaeger sighed and said, "Okay, I gotta ask. Why farming?"

Searcher thought for a moment. "Well, I love being outside and being my own boss."

Jaeger nodded. "Right, I get that."

"And I like that I can pour my heart and soul into what I'm growing—to make sure it becomes exactly what I need it to be," said Searcher. "Something strong, that lasts. A legacy that my son can be proud of."

"Hmm . . . I get that, too," Jaeger admitted.

Searcher fell silent, trying to muster up the courage to ask his dad a tough question.

But he didn't have to ask. Jaeger seemed to read his mind. "You wanna know why I didn't go back when I coulda," said Jaeger, staring straight ahead.

"The thought did cross my mind," said Searcher.

"It's . . . it's because I'm stuck," said Jaeger.

"Stuck?" Searcher wrinkled his brow. "But I thought you said—"

"Yeah, different kind of stuck," Jaeger explained. "You see, I've been an explorer my whole life. Chasing that horizon—that's all I've ever known. Even though it cost me everything: You. Your mom. The last twenty-five years of my life. If I gave up on it, what would I be? *Who* would I be?"

Searcher knew exactly who Jaeger would still be: his dad. But before he could say so, Jaeger's face hardened.

"Well, too old to change now," Jaeger said with a chuckle, before taking the last sip from his bottle. He gazed into the horizon.

"Right," Searcher agreed. His shoulders sagged in disappointment.

Meanwhile, in the cockpit, Meridian was growing tired from hours of piloting the *Venture.* She rubbed her stiff neck just as Splat appeared. "Oh, hi . . . *you,*" she said.

Splat made itself comfortable at the control panel—too comfortable. The little blue creature started fiddling with levers and switches.

"Hey, don't touch that!" Meridian said, scolding it. Her seat zoomed forward and backward as Splat pushed buttons and pulled levers. "Hey! Hey, stop it! Bad Splat!"

When she reached to grab the lever Splat was about to pull, Splat slapped her hand away. She raised an eyebrow and gave Splat her most stern mom look.

Splat squealed and slunk off the controls.

"Mm-hmm," said Meridian smugly. "You tried."

Splat cowered behind the copilot's seat as Ethan stepped into the cabin and sat down beside Meridian. He glanced toward the deck, where Searcher and Jaeger were sharing a drink and chatting. "Hmm, look at that. They're finally getting along," he said in surprise.

"About time, right?" said Meridian.

"Especially since they're basically the same person," said Ethan as both men scratched their behinds and then leaned against the rail, looking like twins.

"Mmm," said Meridian, "don't let your father hear you say that!"

They shared a laugh of their own. Then Meridian cocked her head. "Hey, you wanna take the wheel?" she asked. "I'm dying for a cup of coffee."

Ethan's jaw dropped. "Wait, really?"

"Yeah." Meridian gestured through the windshield. "Just follow the roots."

"Okay," said Ethan. As he slid eagerly into the pilot's seat and reached for the controls, Splat hopped back onto the control panel—a ready and willing copilot.

Ethan eased the *Venture* onward through the beautifully strange world. "Whoa!" he said, marveling at the fact that he was actually *flying* this ship.

Meridian stood behind him with her coffee. "Hmm," she said proudly. "If only Diazo could see you now. . . ."

Ethan glanced up in surprise.

"What?" she said, smiling wide. "You don't think your dad and I talk?"

Ethan laughed nervously.

She took a sip of coffee. "You're doing great," she said, watching him work the controls. "Yeah, just"—she suddenly glanced up through the window—"watch out for that walking landmass!"

A giant cliff with two legs was crossing their path.

"Whoa!" cried Ethan. With his mother's help, he veered the *Venture* around the cliff creature. "And . . . I've got it. See?" he said, trying to sound confident.

When Ethan caught Jaeger and Searcher glaring at him, both gripping the rail for dear life, he hollered, "Sorry, sorry! My bad! We're all good!"

Splat was shaken by the near crash, too. It whined as it slowly got to its feet.

Ethan readily gave up the controls as Meridian

slid back into the pilot's seat. As she eased the ship back to a straight course, she gazed out the window. "Why is this place so weird?" she murmured.

"Eh, I don't know," said Ethan. "I think this place is kind of amazing."

Meridian studied the smile on his face. "I gotta say, Ethan. I've never seen you so happy as you are down here."

Ethan thought about that for a moment. "I guess . . . the farm is so small. The world is so big. I just feel . . . like I'm in my element. I don't know."

Meridian stared at her son as if she were seeing him for the very first time.

"What?" he asked. "Why are you looking at me like that?"

"I can look at you!" she insisted.

"Mom, please don't make it weird," he said, shrinking in his seat.

"Moms can't be weird," she said defensively. "We gave birth to you! We've got rights. I'd like to exercise my right to stare at you . . . uncomfortably."

Ethan gave her an exasperated smile. "No, you have to focus on the road," he said, pointing. "You have to look at the road. You're driving."

"Oh, calm down!" Meridian grew serious again. "I'm just saying, maybe you should keep exploring those feelings. It just might lead you down some interesting paths."

As Ethan considered her words, Meridian settled back in her seat. They fell into a comfortable silence. But it wouldn't last for long.

Chapter Twelve

The *Venture* continued on its course, following the glowing Pando roots into a dark, gray cavern. The world here seemed to be shriveling up and dying, but the Pando roots were strong and thriving.

The Clades gathered in the cockpit and studied the cavern. Splat began to whimper. The pitiful creature leaped from Ethan's shoulder and hid behind his legs.

Hoping to be reassured, Ethan looked to his grandfather, the bravest explorer in the room. But even Jaeger looked concerned. "Are you okay, Grandpa?" Ethan asked.

Jaeger pressed his lips together. "Been down here for twenty-five years," he said solemnly. "And I've never seen anything like this."

Searcher gazed at the thick, glowing roots. "That doesn't make sense," he said. "Pando seems to be getting stronger the deeper we go."

Callisto stared out the window, searching for clues. "If Pando's dying, shouldn't it be getting weaker?" she pointed out.

Splat chattered excitedly. It jumped onto the control panel, trying to get their attention.

"Splat, are you okay?" asked Ethan.

Splat began to act something out.

"Oh, wait," said Searcher. "It's trying to tell us something."

"Are you hungry?" Callisto guessed.

"You need to potty?" tried Searcher.

"Ethan's stuck in a well?" Meridian offered.

"Standing right here, Mom," Ethan pointed out.

Meridian shrugged. "I'm trying, okay? Thing's got no face!"

Splat kept trying to make them understand, frantically gesturing to the window.

"Monsters! Monsters! Monsters!" Caspian shouted, pointing toward Splat.

"Hello? Insensitive," Ethan scolded. "Splat's part of the family now."

"No," Caspian said, his face going slack with fear as he looked out the window. "Monsters!"

Everyone whirled around toward the rear of the ship. Scads of Reapers and winged creatures were charging toward the *Venture*. Callisto grabbed a weapon, prepared to fight.

"Meridian, go!" cried Searcher.

Meridian gunned it to escape the predators. But the ship wasn't fast enough. "I can't outrun them," she cried. "Take cover!"

Searcher hugged Ethan protectively while Jaeger instinctively used his broad body to shield them both.

Any moment now, the beasts would attack. But then . . . they didn't. The group watched as the monsters sailed right past the *Venture*!

Searcher glanced up, confused. "They didn't attack us. Why didn't they attack us?"

Meridian peered through the windshield. "It might have something to do with that," she said in an ominous voice.

A massive cluster of Pando roots converged ahead, wrapped around some sort of pulsating mound. And what looked like thousands of creatures were attacking the roots.

"I think we found the heart of Pando," said Callisto in a grave voice.

Dinosaur-like beasts galloped toward the tangle of Pando roots. Winged creatures attacked it from the air. Reapers lashed at the roots with their tentacle-like tongues. The monsters lunged at the sizzling roots, over and over again, attacking them from the air and the ground.

"What are they doing?" asked Ethan, straining to see.

"They're doing what any pest would do," said Searcher, his brow furrowed. "They're trying to dig into Pando's heart to devour it from the inside!"

"It's fighting for its life out there!" cried Callisto.

Searcher had a sudden realization. "*That's* why our plants are dying up top!" he shouted. "Pando's rerouting all its energy to protect itself right here. Our plant's not sick. It's at war!"

Callisto set her jaw. "Well, let's even the odds," she said.

"Easier said than done," pointed out Jaeger.

"We have Pando," declared Callisto.

"Do you know how much Pando that would take?" cried Jaeger, gesturing toward the masses of creatures ahead.

Callisto whirled around to face him. "You got a better idea?"

"Yeah," Jaeger answered. "We skip this crap carnival and fly to the other side of the mountains."

Callisto put her hands on her hips. "How does that save Pando exactly?" she asked, her eyes flashing.

"It doesn't," Jaeger admitted. "But I lived my whole life without the stuff. You'll be fine."

While Jaeger and Callisto argued about what to

do, Searcher had already hatched a plan. He raced across the room, grabbed a container of Pando pods, and dumped them out on a table. He began crushing the pods and pouring the Pando dust into a launcher.

"Twenty-five years and you still don't get it," Callisto was saying to Jaeger. "We're not dropping Pando just so you can plant your flag. Avalonia is depending on us to save it, and *that's* what we're gonna do."

"I couldn't agree more," Searcher announced, ready to execute his plan. Everyone turned to look as he strode past them toward the deck.

"Dad, what are you doing?" Ethan called.

As the next swarm of Reapers charged by, Searcher took aim with his nozzle and fired. Pando dust streamed out, shocking dozens of Reapers and dropping them to the ground.

"Just like how we do it on our farm," Searcher declared.

Callisto smiled with sudden understanding. "Not bad, Baby Clade!"

She called to her crew. "Listen up. Bring up every crate of Pando from the hull. Looks like we're turning the *Venture* into the world's biggest crop duster!"

The crew members kicked into action, crushing Pando pods, turning harpoon guns into crop-dusting nozzles, and filling a large feeder tank full of Pando dust to power the nozzles.

But as they continued to prepare for battle, Splat raced toward Ethan. The little blue creature had something important to say.

"What is it, Splat?" asked Ethan.

Splat pointed toward the war zone below—at the throbbing Pando-wrapped mound covered with creatures—and then touched Ethan's chest.

"I don't understand," said Ethan. Then he heard his father calling him. "I'm sorry, Splat, but I gotta go."

Ethan hurried toward Searcher, who stood by the deck rail holding two launchers with nozzles. "Yeah, Dad?" asked Ethan.

"Here." Searcher handed him a nozzle. "We came down here to save our farm, and that's what we're gonna do. Together. Side by side."

Ethan stared at the Pando gun in his hands. Somehow, it just didn't feel right. "You know what? I'm—I'm good," he said, handing it back to his father. "I wouldn't even know what to do."

"It's simple," said Searcher. "You just point and spray." He demonstrated how to use the Pando gun.

But Ethan wasn't interested. "This is more your thing, Dad," he said.

"This is *our* thing, Ethan," Searcher argued. "Father and son."

Ethan protested, louder this time. "It just doesn't feel right to me. I don't want to kill all these creatures!"

Searcher paused. "Well," he said thoughtfully, "don't think of it as killing. We're just exterminating some pests trying to destroy our crops. We're *farmers*, Ethan. This is what farmers do." He offered Ethan the launcher again.

But Ethan wouldn't take it. He looked his father straight in the eye and said, "Well, then . . . maybe I'm not a farmer."

Searcher's jaw dropped. "What?"

"I'm not a farmer, Dad," Ethan said sadly, as if admitting it to himself for the first time.

Searcher's face darkened. "Ethan, where is all this coming from? This doesn't sound like you."

"But it *is* me, Dad!" cried Ethan. "This is probably the most me I've ever been. I just feel like I'm in my element when I'm exploring this world."

"Exploring?" Searcher scoffed.

"Well, yeah, I mean . . . ," Ethan stammered. "There's just so much to discover here—"

"Wait, wait. Are you saying . . . you want to be an explorer?" Searcher said, glowering.

When Jaeger overheard the argument, he hurried toward them. "Hey, is everything all right?"

"Is this because of him?" Searcher asked Ethan, gesturing toward Jaeger.

"What? No!" said Ethan.

"It is, isn't it?" said Searcher, his voice rising. "What did you say to Ethan?" He turned to face Jaeger.

Jaeger held up his palms. "I didn't say anything!"

Ethan backed him up. "Dad, it's not Grandpa's fault."

But Searcher wouldn't hear a word of it. "Are you trying to brainwash my son?" He got up in Jaeger's face now, way too close.

"Brainwash?" Jaeger's brow furrowed.

Searcher turned back to Ethan and pleaded with his son. "Ethan, will you trust me?" he said. "You do not want to be like him. The only thing he cares about is himself and conquering those mountains."

Jaeger's heart sank as he took in Searcher's stinging words. His head dropped, and he walked in the other direction.

Searcher took his son by the shoulders. "I know you, Ethan, and this isn't you."

But Ethan had heard enough, too. He spun around and sprinted away from his father.

"Come back here!" Searcher cried. "Ethan!"

When Ethan saw the stream of red creatures flying past the *Venture,* he climbed the deck rail and launched straight off, landing in the stream below.

Chapter Thirteen

Half-horrified and half-angry, Searcher hopped on the nearest skiff, gunned the throttle, and raced after his son.

"Are you crazy?" he hollered as he caught up to Ethan. "Get on this skiff now!"

"Leave me alone!" cried Ethan, storming down the moving red walkway.

"Hey, what is this all about?" Searcher yelled over the buzz of the skiff.

"You, Dad. *You!*" said Ethan.

"Me?"

"You just assume I'll follow in your footsteps, but you never asked me what I wanted."

Before Ethan could march any farther, Searcher zoomed up next to him and pulled him onto the skiff. "You're a kid," said Searcher. "You don't know what you want."

"I know I don't want to be you!" Ethan spat. He glared at his father and then turned away.

The words hit their mark. Searcher suddenly remembered a similar argument, one he'd had with his own father in a cavern strewn with fallen icicles.

He sighed and stopped the skiff in midair, where it floated into the fog. Then he turned sideways so that he and Ethan were sitting hip to hip, facing opposite directions. "My whole life," Searcher said wearily, "I worked so hard to be the exact opposite of my dad. And it looks like I ended up just like him."

Ethan said nothing, but he was listening.

"I just wanted so badly to build you a legacy you can be proud of," said Searcher. "But . . . I mighta got a little caught up in it. I guess . . . I'm just scared of losing you."

Ethan's expression softened as golden light hit his face. "Dad," he said. "Stop talking. Stop talking!"

Searcher sighed. "Ethan, I'm trying to apologize here—"

"Dad!" Ethan interrupted, nudging his dad to turn around. Ethan pointed to the sky.

Searcher turned, prepared to see another weird creature or strange land formation—but what he saw was entirely new. Above them, puffy white clouds parted to reveal a shining sun—and a tapering mountain range.

"Dad," Ethan said hesitantly, "I think we're on the other side of the mountains."

The clouds continued to disperse, revealing what lay beyond the rocky peaks: a vast blue ocean, stretching as far as their eyes could see.

"There's nothing but water out there," murmured Searcher.

No sooner had he said those words than the world beneath their hovering skiff suddenly began to rumble. Nearby, a crumbling cliff split in two, its top half lifting from the bottom—revealing a giant eye blinking open.

"Th-th-that's an eye, right?" Searcher stammered.

"Yeah," Ethan whispered.

"A really, *really* big eye . . . ," Searcher pointed out.

"Yeah," said Ethan again.

Searcher swallowed hard. "And it's looking right at us."

Then Ethan sucked in his breath. "You know what this means, right?"

"It's judging me?" Searcher said, unable to stop staring at the bizarre sight.

"No, if this place has an eye, it has to be attached to a head," said Ethan. "And if this place has a head, that means what we've been traveling through this entire time was its insides!"

Searcher scrunched up his face. "Like its guts and stuff?"

"Okay, yes. Hear me out," Ethan said as he put it all together. "The windy forest that we were in? That's the lungs," he said, remembering the trees that seemed to inhale and exhale. "And the acid lake? That's the stomach!" He waved his hands excitedly.

"And this giant eye must be . . . ," added Searcher, "its eye." It was the best he could come up with at a moment like this.

"The Reapers aren't monsters!" said Ethan, thinking aloud. "They're an immune system."

"What?" Searcher struggled to understand.

"That's what Splat was trying to tell me!" Ethan exclaimed. "This place is alive. It's a living thing! We didn't find the heart of Pando . . ."—he placed his hand on his chest, where Splat had been pointing— "we found an actual heart! And Pando's killing it."

Searcher's eyes widened in realization. He knew exactly what they had to do.

Chapter Fourteen

As Searcher and Ethan sped back into the dark cavern—the chest of this living animal—they saw the *Venture* spraying plumes of green dust from its cannons. The Pando dust was killing the Reapers and flying creatures, dropping them on contact in a shower of sizzles and sparks.

Searcher hit the throttle, and they zoomed toward the *Venture*'s cockpit.

Inside, Meridian sat at the controls, trying to hold the airship steady. But Splat tugged at her arms.

"What are you doing now?" she muttered.

But Splat wouldn't budge. The little blue creature gestured and babbled in a language she couldn't understand. Splat sounded angry now.

"*What?*" Meridian pointed a warning finger at Splat. "I don't know what you just said, but I'm pretty sure it was really inappropriate."

Just then, Searcher and Ethan burst into the cabin.

"Mom!" cried Ethan. "You have to turn this ship around!"

"What?" Meridian raised her eyebrows.

"Mission's over," Searcher explained. "This place is not what it seems."

Overhearing the commotion, Callisto stepped into the cabin with Jaeger and the *Venture* crew close behind. "Is there a problem?" she asked.

"Big problem!" said Ethan.

"Listen, Ethan and I got into this huge fight—" Searcher began.

"Which honestly was kind of my fault. It was really poor timing—" Ethan interjected.

"I also wasn't really in a place to listen—" Searcher admitted.

"So I just jumped off the ship—" Ethan said casually.

"You jumped off the ship?" Meridian exclaimed.

"But he's safe!" said Searcher, resting a hand on her shoulder. "And the next thing we know, we're on the other side of the mountains, staring directly at—"

"A giant eyeball!" they said together.

"What?" Jaeger asked.

"I know, Grandpa. Crazy, right?" said Ethan.

"Do you know what this means?" Searcher asked Callisto, spreading his arms wide.

"Not even remotely," she responded, her face blank.

"It means this place—the world we live on—is a living thing," Searcher said, emphasizing each word.

Callisto chuckled doubtfully. "Hold up. What?"

"*That's* why this place is so weird!" Meridian exclaimed, finally putting it together.

Splat threw out its limbs at Meridian as if to say, "Yes! I *tried* to tell you!"

Searcher turned to Callisto. "Pando's not the miracle plant we thought it was," he explained. "It's a parasite. And we grew that parasite into a monster big enough to destroy our entire world. If we want to survive, Pando has to go."

"So . . . you—the guy who *found* Pando—now want us to *destroy* Pando?" she asked, her voice rising.

"Look, I don't like the sound of this either," Searcher told her. "Especially after what Pando's given us—what it's given me."

Out of the corner of his eye, he saw Jaeger move toward the door. "Dad?" Searcher called, following him out to the catwalk, where Ethan and Searcher had just parked the skiff.

"Dad, wait," Searcher pleaded. "I really need your help here."

Jaeger scoffed. "You're out of your mind."

"Listen," said Searcher, trying to keep his voice calm, "if we don't do something about Pando, the whole world will die. You don't want that to be your legacy."

Jaeger's face turned to stone. "Don't you talk to me about legacy!" he roared. "We were going to reach the other side of the mountains together, father and son. But you quit on me. You quit!" He clenched his jaw and looked his son in the eye. "This was supposed to be our second chance. But now you've ruined it."

Jaeger stepped toward the skiff, but Searcher placed a hand on his shoulder to stop him.

"Dad, I'm sorry," Searcher said.

Jaeger tenderly placed his hand over his son's. Then he brushed Searcher's hand away, turned on his heel, and mounted the skiff.

"Dad, wait!" Searcher said. "Dad!"

But Jaeger didn't say another word before he sped off, leaving Searcher alone on the catwalk.

Dejected but still determined, Searcher returned to the cockpit—and found a nasty surprise.

Callisto had directed crew members to detain

Meridian and Ethan, who now stood at the back of the cabin with their arms held behind their backs.

"Callisto, what are you doing?" Searcher cried, lunging toward his family.

Pulk and Hardy suddenly rushed forward and grabbed Searcher's arm.

"I'm sorry, Searcher," said Callisto, lifting her chin, "but our entire world runs on Pando. We came down here to save it. That plan hasn't changed."

With that, the crew dragged Searcher, Meridian, and Ethan from the room.

"You have no idea what you're doing!" Searcher called. "You're going to destroy Avalonia!"

But before he knew it, he and his family had been pushed into a tiny storage closet. Hardy tossed Splat into the closet, too; slammed the door shut; and turned the lock before marching away.

"You can't do this!" Searcher shouted. He yanked the door handle. "You have to listen to me!"

Searcher dropped to his stomach on the floor.

"What are you doing?" asked Ethan, squirming to make room for his father.

"I'm trying to get a look outside," said Searcher. He pushed his fingers through the gap beneath the door. "Ethan, do you think you can reach your arm under here and up to the door handle?"

"Clearly, no," Ethan said, unamused.

"Wait, what's that noise?" Meridian asked.

Something was scratching at the door. Searcher pressed his cheek against the floor, trying to see below the door. Then a slobbery tongue shot through the gap and licked his face.

"*Ack!* No tongue!" Searcher cried.

The dog barked happily in return.

"Legend!" exclaimed Ethan.

His dog whined and panted, as if wanting desperately to help.

Ethan dropped to the floor beside Searcher. "Hey, boy, hey, open the door!" he prodded. "Yeah, open the door!"

Legend spun in an excited circle, barking all the while.

"Open the door!" Searcher chimed in.

"Come on, Legend," said Meridian. "You can do it!"

The dog stuck his snout beneath the door and rolled onto his back, as if trying to wiggle underneath.

"OPEN THE DOOR!" Searcher finally ordered.

"Can you not yell at my dog?" said Ethan.

"I wouldn't yell if he were actually trained," Searcher grumbled.

"He *is* trained," said Ethan. "He hasn't peed in the house in the last two days."

"We've been on this ship for the last two days," Meridian pointed out.

"And he hasn't peed in the house that entire time," said Ethan, resting his case.

While the family argued, Splat took charge. The creature chattered something that Legend seemed to understand. The dog stood on his haunches and pawed at the handle.

Searcher saw the handle wiggle. "You still have to unlock it," he said, as if Legend could understand. "There's a switch right beside the handle. Legend, see the switch?"

Legend cocked his head and . . . licked the switch.

"What's that sound?" asked Searcher. "Is he licking the switch? Legend, stop licking the switch. STOP LICKING THE SWITCH!"

Fed up with all the drama, Splat suddenly flattened its body to the floor and squeezed beneath it. The little blue creature stretched up and unlocked the door. Splat mimed for Legend how to push the handle down to open the door. Then Splat squeezed back beneath the door to join the Clades in the closet.

Seconds later, Legend pushed the handle down, and the door swung open.

The family looked at Splat, stunned. Then they spilled out of the closet and ran down the hallway.

"Okay, what's the plan?" asked Ethan.

"First thing's first," said Searcher. "Let's get back control of the ship."

Chapter Fifteen

*T*he battle raged on just outside the airship. On the rear deck, Callisto observed with satisfaction as the *Venture* crew operated the giant cannons, blasting every beast in range with deadly Pando dust.

The newly freed Clades crept through the galley toward the cockpit, where Caspian was alone at the controls. As Searcher, Meridian, and Ethan charged through the door, they waved their weapons—Searcher's Pando picker and a mop and broom stolen from the storage closet.

"Ahh!" The Clades shouted their battle cry.

Caspian whirled around from the control panel, an instruction manual in his hands. "Ahh!" he cried back. "I am not qualified to fly this ship!" He tossed over the instruction manual without a fight. "It's all yours. Piloting is hard!" he said as he raced out of the cockpit.

The family shared a surprised glance.

"Huh. That was easy," said Ethan, sounding a tad disappointed.

Meridian sat in the pilot's seat and placed her hands confidently on the wheel, ready to go . . . somewhere. But where?

"Okay, what now?" she asked.

Searcher considered their options. "So Pando defenses are keeping those creatures from destroying it from the inside," he said, thinking aloud. "But if I can dig a hole for them—"

"They can take care of the rest," Meridian said, finishing his thought. Her eyes brightened. "That could work!"

Searcher grinned. It was a good solution—the only solution. And he was ready to take action.

Meridian gave him a kiss. "I'll keep Callisto off your back," she said. "You keep our son safe out there."

Searcher shook his head. "What? He's not coming with me."

Meridian raised an eyebrow and signaled for him to turn around. "Tell him that."

Searcher looked out the window and saw Ethan and Splat riding on the back of a flying creature. It flapped its enormous red wings, but it didn't buck them off.

"You coming?" Ethan called.

Searcher wasn't about to let Ethan go down there

alone. He kissed Meridian and grabbed his Pando picker from behind the pilot's seat. Then he charged out of the cockpit and took a running leap onto the flying beast.

Meridian watched proudly as Searcher threw an arm around his son and held the Pando picker above his head, looking like a superhero. Ethan and Searcher blew her a kiss. Then they rode the flying beast straight toward the battlefield, as if they'd been riding creatures like this all their lives.

With a deep breath, Meridian turned the wheel, sending the *Venture* in the opposite direction.

Back on the rear deck, Jaeger, Callisto, and her crew were still spraying the creatures with Pando dust.

"Remember, everybody," Callisto said, "Avalonia's depending on us."

Suddenly, the flying creature soared overhead in a flurry of red wings. Everyone on the deck ducked as it flew past.

"Was that Searcher and Ethan?" Callisto asked, thoroughly confused.

Then the airship veered, and everyone grabbed the rail for balance.

"What's happening?" Pulk asked, watching as they moved away from the battlefield below.

A flash of realization crossed Callisto's face. "They took the bridge," she said. "Come on!"

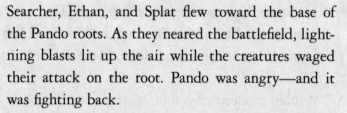

Meanwhile, Jaeger had finally made it to his destination. He parked his skiff. Just a few more steps and he would find himself on the other side of the mountains!

He paused, preparing to meet his destiny at last. But before he could move forward, the earth began to shake. The entire world rumbled around him. He looked around, wondering what was happening.

Had Searcher been right?

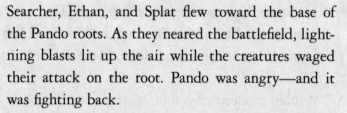

Searcher, Ethan, and Splat flew toward the base of the Pando roots. As they neared the battlefield, lightning blasts lit up the air while the creatures waged their attack on the root. Pando was angry—and it was fighting back.

Searcher shielded his eyes against the bright flashes, looking for the best spot to enact his plan. "There!" he shouted. "Where all the roots converge. If the Reapers attack that, the rest of the plant will crumble."

Ethan nodded and steered the winged beast toward their target. He landed the creature with ease.

Once their feet were on the ground, Searcher

turned to his son. "You and Splat round up every creature you can find and send them my way," he instructed. "I'll do the rest."

"You got it, Dad," Ethan said, his eyes sparkling with excitement.

Searcher wrapped his son in a hug. "Ethan, I am sorry if I ever made you think you had to be a farmer to make me proud. I am *always* proud of you."

"I know, Dad," Ethan said, squeezing him back. "I know."

Searcher watched as Ethan ran off, with Splat on his shoulders, to summon the Reapers. Then he turned and faced the enormous tangle of Pando roots.

Lightning lit up the darkness. Searcher was all alone. And he had work to do.

He squared off against the sizzling roots. He took a deep breath and raised his Pando picker. With all his strength, he drove the sharp blade into the thick roots.

Thwack!

A bolt of electricity shot from where the blade hit the Pando root, but Searcher dodged it just in time. This wasn't going to be easy, he realized. But he had to keep fighting—no matter what. He raised his Pando picker to strike again.

"Meridian! Open this door!" Callisto demanded as the crew pounded on the cockpit door.

Meridian held her focus and gripped the steering wheel. "Sorry, can't hear you!" she called. "Too busy being awesome in here."

"Don't worry, President Mal," Caspian reassured her. "I got this." He took a step back and bellowed a full-throated battle cry, throwing his body against the door before landing in a crumpled heap on the floor.

"Did it move even a little bit?" he called up to them.

Callisto and Pulk rolled their eyes and then together kicked the door open themselves. *CRASH!*

"Let go of those controls," Callisto ordered.

Meridian shrugged and let go of the steering wheel. The ship immediately lurched sideways, sending the crew flying into the wall.

"Grab the controls! Grab the controls!" Callisto shouted.

"Geez, make up your mind," said Meridian casually before righting the ship. Then she hit the throttle, sending the *Venture* blasting forward and knocking Callisto and the crew off their feet. Legend barked with glee as he slid back and forth across the floor on his behind.

"I think she's messing with us," Caspian observed.

Callisto gave him a look as if to say "Gee, you think so?" She pulled herself to her feet and charged toward the pilot's seat. "Stop!" she told Meridian.

"No prob," Meridian said applying the breaks. "We're here."

Confused, Callisto and her crew looked out the windshield. Nobody said a word as they took in the scene before them.

"Searcher was right," Callisto said, breaking the silence. "That's not the heart of Pando. That's an actual heart."

Meridian nodded, grateful that they finally understood. "Now let's hope he's not too late."

Chapter Sixteen

Searcher drove his Pando picker into the root once again. *ZAP!* A giant bolt of electricity burst from the plant. It struck Searcher in the chest. As he reeled from the blow, another blast hit his leg. He crumpled to the ground.

He smelled smoke and could see charred burns on his clothing. But he had to keep fighting. As long as Pando lived, there was no other choice.

Searcher got to his hands and knees and tried to muster the energy to stand. That's when he heard a familiar voice in the distance.

"On your feet, Searcher," the voice said gruffly.

Searcher squinted as a hulking silhouette approached through the smoke. "Dad?" Searcher said.

Jaeger reached out a hand and helped Searcher to his feet. "Let's do this together," he said. "Father and son."

He pulled out his flamethrower and tore it apart,

extracting the climbing hammers that he had used to fashion the weapon's body.

With grim determination, Searcher and Jaeger marched toward the root side by side. Lightning struck the ground all around as they prepared to tear into the Pando root with their tools.

Searcher watched as Jaeger awkwardly clawed at the root with his hammer, as if building a sandcastle. Searcher stopped him and demonstrated how to rear back and strike the ground with his tool. Jaeger grinned at his son proudly and gave it a try, thrusting his climbing hammers into the ground.

As they continued to dig, the *Venture* came into view overhead.

"There!" shouted Meridian, spotting Searcher and Jaeger ramming their tools into the ground in unison as lightning flashed around them.

Out of the corner of his eye, Jaeger saw a glowing pulse of energy building in the Pando roots that formed the ceiling of this strange world.

"Searcher?" Jaeger called.

Searcher's eyes met Jaeger's. They both knew: it was now or never.

"Keep digging," Searcher told his father.

They lifted their tools over their shoulders. Then, together, they cleaved the root, finally exposing the plant's fragile interior.

BOOM!

An enormous blast hit both men square in the chest. As Searcher hit the ground, he saw Ethan and Splat charging toward him with an army of Reapers in their wake.

The Reapers swarmed into the gash that Searcher and Jaeger had carved for them. The mother root began to disintegrate while Reapers tore it to shreds from the inside out. More creatures joined, coming to finish the fight.

"That's a Clade boy right there!" Jaeger shouted, helping Searcher to his feet.

"We did it!" Searcher said, catching his breath. "Aha! We did it!"

Ethan grinned. But as he looked around, he wasn't so sure. "You did it, right?"

The three Clades looked around at the eerily silent landscape. Everything remained gray, still, and lifeless.

Just then, Meridian zoomed in on a skiff. "Searcher!" she called, hopping off and running to her husband.

Searcher squeezed her tight. "We were too late," he said with a sinking heart. "It's over."

The group took another silent moment to look around before they climbed onto the skiff, ready to return to the *Venture*.

But as the skiff rose into the air, Ethan pointed. "Dad, look!"

Below them, thousands of little round nubby creatures rolled and scurried across the scorched earth. The golden creatures emitted a soft, healing glow. Wherever they passed, the blackened earth came back to life—vibrant and colorful.

Suddenly, a thumping sound filled the cavern. *Tha-thump, tha-thump, tha-thump. . . .* The giant heart, now free of the Pando roots that Searcher and Jaeger had destroyed, began to beat.

Chapter Seventeen

By the time the Clades had returned to the *Venture*, the strange world around them—the body of the living animal that they had just saved—had come alive with a beautiful, radiant energy.

But now it was time to say goodbye.

Leaving Splat was hardest of all. Ethan hugged his little blue friend, who hugged back by wrapping all its arms around Ethan. As the *Venture* took to the air, Ethan waved until Splat was out of view. Even Legend barked a goodbye.

"All right," Meridian announced from the pilot's seat, "next stop—warm showers, hot coffee, and angry masses. Who's ready to go home?"

Searcher was more than ready to return to Avalonia. But then he saw his dad's face. While the others celebrated, Jaeger stared solemnly out the window, deep in thought.

"Actually," Searcher said to Meridian, "I'd like to make one stop. For my dad."

Jaeger looked up in surprise.

Meridian nodded with understanding and hit the throttle. Soon the ship was flying toward an opening high above.

Moments later, Jaeger gazed out over the rail of the ship's deck. The ocean stretched out before them, an endless sea of blue. At last, Jaeger knew what lay beyond the mountains.

Meridian and Callisto stood on the other side of the deck, staring at the jaw-dropping scene below them.

As Searcher stepped beside his father, Jaeger sighed happily. "I spent my whole life wondering about this moment—what it'd be like, what it'd look like, what it'd . . . feel like," he said softly.

"And how does it feel?" asked Searcher.

"Feels . . . perfect," said Jaeger. He wrapped one arm around Searcher and the other around Ethan and Meridian, pulling them in for a hug. Then he reached for Callisto, bringing her in, too.

Never one to miss a group hug, Legend bounced across the deck to join them.

Together, as a family, they stared in awe at the endless sea.

Epilogue

In the year since the Clade family had returned home, Avalonia had changed greatly. Instead of relying on Pando for energy, the city used hydropower generated by the flow of water coming down from the mountains.

Now Meridian flew high overhead in a new kind of machine that strapped onto her back and allowed her glide through the air like a graceful winged insect. Down below, Searcher grew fruits and vegetables on his farm instead of Pando, and Jaeger worked by Searcher's side. Now that Jaeger had fulfilled his legacy, he could help Searcher with his own—Clade Family Farms.

As for Ethan? He was returning to the strange world he had left behind a year ago—to revisit the living animal that Avalonia rested upon, with Diazo, Kardez, and Azimuth this time. There was still so much to explore—and a lot of dead Pando roots to clean up!

As they made the journey, Ethan wrote his dad a letter.

Dear Dad,
The world's changed. It continues to change. And though we can't live like we did in the past, we've now given ourselves a better chance at the future.
The best legacy we can leave is making a present worth opening tomorrow. You really are a hero, Dad. Thank you for everything you've given me. I'll do my best to live up to your legacy. I hope I make you proud.
Love always,
Your son

When they arrived in that strange, beautiful underground world, Ethan couldn't wait to introduce Diazo to his old friend, Splat. There it was! The little creature squealed and scurried up to Ethan, as if it had been waiting for him to return at any moment.

Splat hopped onto Ethan's shoulder, and Diazo rested his head on the other. Ethan was following his own path now—not his father's, and not his grandfather's. He was forging his own way and creating his own legacy, at last.